Storm Warnings

Storm Warnings

stories of love and sorrow

TOM HENIGHAN

Stone Flower Press, Ottawa
Cover photo: Tom Henighan
Production Design: Jen Hamilton
Printed by CreateSpace

**Library and Archives Canada Cataloguing in
Publication**

Henighan, Tom, author,
  Storm Warnings/ Tom Henighan
Fiction
ISBN 978-0-9919073-6-6   (paperback)

For Ken and Elisabeth Finch

*It's not the days we remember,
but the moments.*

Cesare Pavese

TABLE OF CONTENTS

Enemies of Culture

This is the story of how I came close to getting culture, of how I was saved at an early age from spending my nights at the opera, at Carnegie Hall, or from living with those cool dudes down in SoHo. It could have been pretty awful that life, and sometimes, gearing up for the Saturday football, or nursing a beer while I take in a Yankee game, the old days come back to me and I shudder and thank God for keeping me clear of all those finer things of life that some people seem to be so hung up on....

I was born in the big city of course, but when we were kids my dad took it into his head to get a farm. The place was way up the Hudson, a wooden frame house with twenty-five acres on some scrub land beyond Newburgh.

Dad got a deal on it and he had some idea that he was going to get rich on those ragged fields, that bit of bush he was clearing out a little faster than it grew. As far back as I can remember my brother Charlie and myself used to have to haul ourselves up and help Dad with the milking and the chores. We complained of course, but it wasn't such a bad life. After a while Mom got an Avon route in the area, and she brought in a little extra money. She and Dad also became Witnesses about that time, so we had to get another car, because Mom at least was always on the road, either peddling the perfume and stuff, or dishing out the fire and brimstone. (Later, Dad sold most of his cows and tried to start a snowmobile business, and when it didn't do so well he gave up religion and started drinking. Mom kicked him out, but he came back one weekend when she was off spreading the Word and burned the house down. So much for fire and brimstone).

All that happened later, when Charlie and I were bustin' into our teens, but bad as it was, it didn't compare with what overtook us in the seventh grade. That was in the small school they had then on the long road that still runs between Newburgh and Walden. The school was a one-storey stone dump, with a little old-fashioned bell suspended up above the tin roof, and a kind of playground enclosed by chicken wire and some cedar bush at the back. The inside was divided into five or six rooms: besides the two big classrooms, there were a couple of teachers' offices and the usual washrooms. The place handled four grades at that time, ranging from five to eight, which they did by a little juggling and makeshift and to be honest the teachers were no great hot stuff.

There was Mrs. Gallinger, who we called the Mule, a stubborn old gray-faced lady who walked around like she was in a strait jacket, never raised her voice, but had you in the wrong every time and let you know it. Also Mr. Crawford, old Crowface, who never smiled once and had a weird funny eye-twitch, but God help you if you let on you noticed. Then there was Preacher, a huge bellied country sod who couldn't snap his fingers without huffing and wheezing. He had a real smooth voice he was proud of and he liked to lecture everyone about how they would never get ahead unless they had a well-rounded education. He was the living proof, I guess.

You can see there were problems, but by the time Charlie and me made the seventh grade, we pretty well had everything sorted out. For one thing, we were the biggest kids in school, except for Dutchy Brink, who was clumsy and pretty thin between the ears and didn't count. Charlie and me started out with an advantage because of my Uncle Gene, a big football star at the time. He was actually a second-string defensive tackle for the Giants, but after he came to the school one time to talk about "sports and education", courtesy of some beer company, Charlie and me had it made. Even the teachers were impressed, and whenever they wanted to get anything across (especially Preacher) they would look down at us as if we were some kind of chosen princes and nod their heads and say: "Isn't that true on the playing field, boys?"—as if we knew a damned thing about it.

We had to walk to school of course, from the crossroads down near Salter's Quarry almost all the way to the Church Road, but we had it good. We would just grab hold of some little grade five or sixer and get him to carry our books and lunch for us. Usually they didn't mind—it was even a kind of honour—but if they gave us any trouble we would strip off their belts and tie 'em up to the old cemetery fence and tell 'em we were gonna leave 'em there for the fossy-jaws to finish them off. (The fossy-jaws were creatures with big fangs that came out of the churchyard at night and ripped people apart—they made me think of one or two Greenbay linebackers I got to watch later).

As for the girls, there were a few pretty ones, and they thought Charlie and me were O.K., to say the least, though it was mostly stuff goin' on in the summer at the pond, foolin' around under water and that kind of thing, with their Moms always breathing down their necks.

Those were the good days all right, but you know what they say, the honeymoon has to end sometime. It hit us just like it hit every baseball fan when the Dodgers moved to LA, or the when the Russians swallowed all those countries and started creaming our guys in the Olympics. And even though we were in like Flynn, thanks to Uncle Gene, all of a sudden in the seventh grade everything was suddenly shot to hell.

It was those two ladies who did it. They'd moved in sometime in the middle of July or August, buying out Sam Razak's place that had been empty since the old gent died the previous winter. As houses go, it was nothing special, a little stone job he had daubed over with blue paint on one side to cheer it up and make you forget the brambles and scrub where old lady Razak used to have her garden. I think he might have put a new bathroom in a few years before and sold the planks and timbers of the wrecked barn, so that the next field looked a little less like a junkyard.

The house was set sideways quite close to the Walden Road, but it had one feature, which, looking back, I see must have impressed those two ladies: all along the road, practically hiding the house, was a spread of wild rose bushes, old-fashioned country roses, which, for some reason, (maybe because his dead wife had planted them) the old bugger had never hacked down.

There were two of them, as I say, Miss Briscoe and Miss Dowling, a couple of old-maid school teachers, as I heard, retiring from Boston. I remember when we were playing ball in a cut field up toward the Quarry that summer I first saw them, tooling along in that funny English car they had. Of course we didn't pay much attention. We were having a good time and enjoying ourselves that summer, not caring that September was zooming up at us faster than a jet-propelled racer, while those two old girls were busy getting the blue paint blasted off the house, trimming the rose bushes, planting shrubs all over the place, and having the inside cleaned and papered over, so that when their furniture and things (including a monstrous big piano) finally arrived, there was a new sight to see on the old road.

A little later, I heard, or Charlie did, something about them giving a fancy tea party. But then Mom, who hadn't been invited, dropped in on them with her pamphlets and perfume and came back crazy about the monster Bible they had showed her, a book printed with old-fashioned letters at the head of each verse, and set on a big stand, underneath a stained glass picture of David playing the harp for Bathsheba. Mom was impressed by the newcomers and I guess one of the school board members, who must have been at the party, was too—because by the time school started that September (in what by rights should have been just one big fun year for Charlie and me) the two of them had been hired to teach music and art appreciation to us poor kids, no less than twice a week, rain or shine.

And that was when our troubles began. I remember that first September morning like it was yesterday. Right after the Pledge of Allegiance the Mule gets up and makes a big to-do about introducing this lady that was standing right there beaming on us like a lighthouse from a cliff. It was Miss Briscoe, with her hard staring eyes and her sharp nose, that red hair all trimmed and permed, and her made-up cheeks spotted redder than a cow's tit.

"Miss Briscoe will be introducing you to the beauty of art," explained the Mule, holding her narrow shoulders kinda stiff when she said it, as if she was announcing something in a big courtroom. "I expect you all to pay close attention," Mrs. Gallinger went on, with a little prim smile at the hussy standing next to her, "because, for many of you, this may be the opportunity of a lifetime."

"An opportunity to sleep," muttered Charlie, just a little too loud, and let fly a hot one. Several kids groaned and there was a few fits of giggling from the girls sitting almost right under Miss Briscoe's nose.

Well, they say that tigers move quickly, but I want to tell you that lady sprang down the aisle and was at Charlie's seat before the smirk left my poor brother's face. She took hold of one ear with her right hand and started pulling up and twisting, while her left hand, clutching tight to some postcards, smacked down hard on his bare neck.

For just one second I could see that Charlie had an impulse to stand right up and take a swing at her—but it was only for a second: he knew what Dad (and maybe the cops) would have done to him if he had punched a lady teacher.

"You *goose!*" she cried out in her shrill voice. "You

silly, silly country goose! Don't you dare to make fun of me, don't you even think of such a thing! I'm here to teach you, do you understand, to bring some of the light of culture into your miserable deprived lives. Now just you take a look at *that*!"

With a grand wave of her hand she slapped a card down hard on Charlie's desk, a picture postcard that she showed off as if it was the ace of spades turned up trumps for some big jackpot.

At the same time, she had let go of poor Charlie's mauled ear, and he was rubbing it over and over, real gingerly, a baffled, stunned look on his face, while he stared down at that postcard and seemed about to puke or just bawl, I don't really know which.

"*That*," announced Miss Briscoe, with a mighty toss of her head, "*that* is "The Laughing Cavalier" by Frans Hals. Take a good look at it, you silly goose, and try to realize that it's ART, REAL ART, something of which you have no inkling now, but which I'm here to instruct you in *class*!" she cried out—and everyone jumped—"take out paper and crayons—at once!"

She strutted back up the aisle, as Mrs. Gallinger looked on in open-mouthed astonishment. Within minutes each of us had one of those little postcards, and with crayons and paper were busy trying to imitate "The Night Watch", "Whistler's Mother", "The Blue Boy" or "The Angelus", while Miss Briscoe, coloured chalk showering around her, was scribbling like mad on the blackboard explaining to us all the fine points of the pictures and telling us about all the terrible things that the poor artists had to suffer to get them done.

Well, take my word for it, we suffered too. Yes sir, our poor half-paralyzed country paws groped around on the paper, squiggling and jiggling out comic-strip cavaliers, aging mothers with hair like tangled wire and hands like swollen mittens, praying peasants resembling human mushrooms, and a few madonnas coloured like turnips and holding pastry babies with beady little stuck-on eyes.

It was quite a session. I remember crouching there, my knees knocking together, afraid that fierce lady would take after me. She'd hopped around the room, bustin' out with whoops and screams, mostly complaining about how awful our stuff was, what a bunch of silly geese we were and so on, and my real terror was that she would grab hold of my ear and twist, because Charlie still sat there trembling, with bowed head, all the fight gone right out of him— the first full-fledged victim of Art that the Walden

District School had ever seen.

It was a long walk home and the worst thing was that we knew Thursday was only the day after tomorrow. As we drifted past that little stone house, we couldn't talk sports or swear or throw stones, as we usually did; we just wished we had a few cans of paint handy and the nerve to use them on those fresh-scrubbed walls.

The next day was almost like a holiday; we hadn't enjoyed school so much in years, but when Thursday morning came around we were tense. We hung in the yard out back as long as we could and watched for that other one. Pretty soon she drove up, just before the bell rang, and we saw the Preacher going out with Dutchy Brink to meet her.

"What the hell is Dutchy doing?" asked Charlie, in some kind of sweat already.

Miss Dowling wasn't at all like the art lady. She was real stocky, though not fat, with short hair and big clunky shoes. With her plain skirt she wore a man's black jacket and a white shirt tied by a funny choker at the neck. You could see she had trouble keeping back the moustache, and her beady eyes darted around everywhere like she was restless to start something.

As she stood smiling and shaking Preacher's hand,

old Dutchy was hauling some kind of big machine out of the trunk of her car.

"A phonograph," said Charlie, with a huge sigh of relief. I guess he figured she couldn't slam his neck with a record player.

After a real slimy introduction by the Preacher, Miss Dowling explained things. There was no whooping and screeching and bouncing around—anyway, the class was just holding its breath. She stood there quite solid and her voice came up like the low end of a barbershop quartet.

"There is music," she said, "and there is *music*. It is up to us to learn to know and love the best. Most of you, I greatly fear, have been deprived of those great classics, which can be truly described as the music of heaven on earth. It will be my pleasure during the year to remedy that deprivation."

She paused, but Charlie didn't open his trap in the slightest; he barely looked round and caught my eye and I could see he was thinking just as I was: *what in hell is this woman talking about?*

Well, that was pretty much the last peaceful moment that whole morning. For the next couple of hours the walls of the room were just about blasted down, like old Jericho's, by a whole bunch of screaming and bawling and thumping that made not the least bit of sense to anybody, not even to Jenny Calvert, who had been studying piano since the first day she fell out of her crib. LP records had just been introduced back then, and there was almost no limit to the torture that lady could inflict on us kids. But whatever she put on the machine, Miss Dowling would always point out that it (or he or she or them) being the greatest that had ever been, or ever could be, we ought to get down on our knees and thank God for having inspired it (or he or she or them) in the first place.

There was some lady called Lily Ponds (I guess it was a pseudonym, or maybe she was sponsored by a company) who was singing some kind of song where she was supposed to be crazy, or else she thought she was a bell—I can't remember now, but that was awful.

There was some Finnish guy who wrote a thing called "Wallstreets". It was gloomy as hell, so I guess he must have lost his shirt.

There was a Russian who imitated cannons and another who did bumblebees, and if I'm not mistaken, one who even did a flea.

There was a whole parcel of Germans, damned if I could tell one from the other, except for that da-da-da-DA thing.

"Fate knocking on the door," Miss Dowling explained, although it might as well have been a bill collector.

There were a few Italians too—you guessed it, with Caruso leading the pack. Probably all waving their arms like crazy and howling, upset because they killed their daughters or their best friends, or their girls ran off with some circus man—but thank God, it wasn't TV.

That was one terrible morning, and when something went wrong with the phonograph needle Miss Dowling said anyway it was time for us to sing. So she made the boys all stand on one side and the girls on the other and we were Hansels and they were Gretels and we all had to clap our hands and tap our toes and skip around—it was positively embarrassing.

"Well," Charlie said later, at lunchtime, "at least she doesn't pull your ears."

"No," I said, "but mine hurt anyway."

I didn't want to spoil his relief, but after a couple of hours of all that screeching and howling and thumping, why would she have to bother?

So that was the end, before they even began, of all the swell times we expected to have in the good old seventh grade. I tell you those culture lessons came whizzing round so fast the whole week seemed to be Tuesdayed and Thursdayed to death. In the end we decided that one lady was just as bad as the other, too: for old Miss Briscoe would fly off the handle and start her ear-pulling whether you provoked her or not, just for the sake of hearing herself screech, I guess; while Miss Dowling kinda stood there and leaned on you like she wanted to flatten you, and if you so much as shifted when one of her precious howlers or thumpers was going on, why she'd stop the music and make you listen to the damned thing all over again.

It wasn't long before those ladies got the idea that Charlie and me were supposed to be the big shots in that class. It seems that they couldn't wait to put us down then, to make fun of everything we liked, especially football and country music. One day Miss Dowling caught me dozing through some terrible singing stuff, some guy whose name I swear was Suzie bawling away in German about some kid who scared himself to death riding out with his dad.

"I suppose you exhausted yourself playing hockey all evening, young man," she pipes up, after standing me in front of the class and shooting me down with four or five questions there was no way I could answer. "Well, all I can say is that as far as

I'm concerned ice hockey is a game for *savages*," she told us in that smooth low-down voice of hers. "Considering, in fact the foul language in the rink and the rowdy exhibitions in the stands, I might even be excused for calling it a game for pigs!"

She babbled along for a while and then sat me down without chewing me out any more, but it was too late. At recess, right after, that wise guy, Bobby Nairn, who was jealous because Maggie Grant liked me, called me "Piggy". Naturally, I beat the crap out of him, but it was no good. Pretty soon, nearly all the kids, and even Charlie, were calling me Piggy. My real name, which is Sterling, somehow got lost in the shuffle, I guess.

Everything was going to the dogs pretty fast, so I kept trying to get off going to school on those Tuesdays and Thursdays. I begged Dad to let me help him out on those mornings, but he was beginning to get into the snowmobile business at the time and he wasn't too interested in hauling himself up at sunrise to do chores. (Actually, he spent most of those mornings just flipping through catalogues figuring out what he was going to blow all our family savings on).

One day I tried something out on Mom. I got hold of a hot water bottle and laid it on my head until I was pretty steamy, then I ran to her and told her I was burning up, I had a temperature, I was much too sick to go to school.

At first she looked worried, but then she hauled out her thermometer and found out I was normal after all.

"Do I have to go to school today, Mom, do I really have to? I asked her.

"You sure do, don't be silly," she told me.

"Couldn't I stay home just this once, just this morning? I'll go along in the afternoon all right. I know I'll feel much better then."

She looked at me like she had understood something after all. Then she thought for a while and finally said:

"Well, I guess it wouldn't hurt if you took just one morning off—though it isn't really right, and it has to be only on one condition."

Just when I was ready to whoop with joy comes a condition.

"What do I have to do, then?" I asked her.

"Well, I was thinking you might like to go on my rounds with me and talk to some of them new folks over by Wallkill about the Bible."

I flopped down into a chair. I thought for a minute, then I told her:

"Well, come to think of it, I guess the bad spell I had is more or less gone away. I guess I'm well enough for school after all."

She didn't crack a smile, so I went off to tell Charlie that my plan was a miserable failure. I never could see ringing doorbells to remind people that the world was coming to an end. Art was pretty bad, I figured, but as for religion—it was even worse.

So we just suffered and suffered, until finally, came a chance for revenge.

It was Halloween, and everybody kind of expected that we were going to go round and raise hell all the way from the Church road to the old swimming hole. I don't really know which of us got the idea first: it maybe just came to us, like one of those inspirations from heaven that got all those painters and music folks going. At any rate Charlie and me agreed we were going to pay back those two ladies for the terrible torture they had put us through since day one.

We decided to dress up as commandos; it was easy enough to find all kinds of surplus military stuff around—khaki shirts, leather belts, helmets and boots—and by the time we were finished we looked pretty scary, I guess. Along the way we picked up a bag of flour and the girls fixed us up with long stockings, which we packed up with the flour and knotted at one end to make nice bombs.

It was a cold night and we got a ride to the crossroads, then walked along over the streaky snow to Razak's. Sure enough, the lights were on. Some little kids we met told us they had dropped in there and come away with a bagful of candies—jelly babies, salt water taffy, Turkish delights, and other kinds of stuff that nobody in his right mind would want to eat. But we didn't care about the candy. We ducked in along the cedars, like we were stalking the place (which we were) and finally got to the edge of the driveway, so that we could see the house lit up, with shadows behind the windows, the place just waiting for us to stir something up at the front door.

As I told you, the building was set sideways, and we crept along the driveway, real happy there was no damned dog to deal with. From inside came some awful piano music and I looked over at Charlie, who had blackened his face just like I had, and we screwed up our eyes and made like we would vomit.

We'd worked out the plan in advance. Charlie scooted across the front steps through the glare of the coach light and ducked into the shadows on the other side. I crept closer and waited for him to get set. Then I counted to three, jumped right up and rang the doorbell.

There was a little pause and the music cut out completely. I could almost feel the old ladies swishing in our direction to play high and mighty to the little kids they expected to find outside. Suddenly, the front door swung open; there was more light and a warm blast of air, and I called out in a crazy cuckoo kind of voice: "Anything for Halloween?"

I could just make out Miss Dowling in some kind of long dress floating up there in the doorway. Then she turned and called out: "Oh come and see, Harriet, the little urchins are playing a game with us."

The other one started to peek over her shoulder. "*Now!*" I cried loud and flung out my sock-bomb.

At the same time I saw Charlie's bomb come flying, like a white worm turning over and over.

SMACK! SMACK! the bombs went, and they sounded loud as hell.

The doorway exploded with powder, a little cloud puffed out, and there was one of the stockings twined limp around the coach light.

Up until that moment I had been carried along by the excitement, just aching to get after those ladies, but now that it was done, I was suddenly scared.

The ladies stood there twisting and squirming, covered with powder, choking, and squinting hard to see who'd gone after them. Then Miss Briscoe bawled in a hurt voice: *"No! Nothing, nothing at all for Halloween!"* and slammed the door vicious and hard.

I couldn't move—I had no breath in me—but Charlie stumbled past me, broke into the driveway and ran. I dragged myself up and ran after him.

"They'll call the police, they're sure to call the police!" Charlie screamed at me as we slipped, stumbled and broke away down the road. The cold air bit our faces; I thought my heart would bust out of my chest, but we ran without stopping—we ran in sheer terror—and finally made it back to the farm.

We couldn't face anyone, but luckily Mom was out, so we crept up to our room and got ourselves cleaned up. "They'll tell on us, I know they will," wailed Charlie as we crawled into bed. "I saw that old red-headed vulture looking out of the window."

The funny thing was, he was right. Somehow they had caught sight of us running, or else made a good guess, but they didn't call the police, they called Dad.

Now Dad didn't have much truck with all that

music and art stuff, but he sure was a great one for discipline. So it was out to the barn for the worst strapping I ever remember, until Mom heard our screaming and bawling and came running out to save us.

We had to write apologies longhand on the best paper and take those ladies a bunch of fancy flowers and a few dozen of the best farm eggs, and of course Mom threw in a chicken for good measure. She was afraid they would go to the police, or else sue us for assault and battery.

The worst thing, though, was facing those two, standing there while they forgave us, and told us how much we'd disappointed them.

Things quietened down after that. The funny thing was they seemed to lay off us from then on, as if somehow what we did had really gotten through to them. But that didn't make us any happier. We almost wished they would go after our scalps, twist our ears, or at least show us that things were back to normal, after all.

So that's how what ought to have been the best year of our school time turned into just about the worst. But there was one mercy: we didn't have to go through it all over again. It seemed that one of the ladies had a rich sister in Boston, and when she suddenly died they inherited her house and so moved right back into the big city. I guess they had had enough of trying to civilize the likes of us.

My brother and me couldn't believe our good luck. What with that culture stuff out of the way things in school went on just beautiful again. We were playing better and better football and basketball and hockey, and went to high school on it, and even though neither of us ever made the big time in any sport, it was a great life while it lasted. Later, of course, Charlie went out west to work for a KFC place; he's doing pretty well and every once in a while, as a joke, he sends along one of those nice plaster gifts they used to give away, and writes something on it, like "busted Greek" or "Blue Boy's brother, Whitey".

As for me, I've made my whole life in football. With a little help from Uncle Gene I even got to work for the Giants for a few seasons. Nothing much, just a locker room job, but that was good enough to fix me up with my high school later. In fact, I'm now what they call a fixture at the old place and as the coach says: "Piggy, I just wouldn't know what to do without you!"

I'm happy, I've got steady work, and like most people who make a living in the sports racket, I don't have to bother with culture.

Even so, once in a while, as I'm driving to a game, or riding the bus with the boys, I'll think all of a sudden—Lord knows why—of "The Laughing Cavalier", or "Whistler's Mother." Or else by mistake somebody will flip onto one of those FM classical music stations and out will come some screeching and howling, or a blast of sound that sets my palms sweating and raises the goose-pimples up and down my back.

So I guess I'm in a rut, or maybe I've got a phobia or something. Whatever it is, I figure it's no good trying to fight it. Just as long as I live, just as long as I remember those God-awful days in the seventh grade, I know I'll be an enemy of culture.

Hotel Paradise

I lived with Steppenwolf, Sam, and Sam's St. Bernard, Lucky, on Quadra for a while during the sixties. When the beaches there got too crowded we moved on, to the west side of the big island. We trekked shoreward past the roads and built lean-tos in the woods, where we stashed clothes, booze and smokes. But we lived most free in the canoes, on the ocean, pushing ourselves as far as we could go.

Mornings we would take off, letting the shore drift away: for hours we would swing the wave gullies, always on the lookout for eagles on the land side and whales out at sea. We rode the big waves, watching the woods dim to shadows, our arms nearly falling off with weariness. Mostly, we were naked; the wind touched our bodies. It was a good life.

Sometimes, though, we pushed it too far; we got reckless. Steppenwolf, who went away often, liked to let go when he came back to the beach. This meant danger, for he was only twenty-two, tall and strong, with a violence held so tight inside him that it would sometimes fix you speechless when you saw it in his cold blue eyes. Steppenwolf loved to take chances—anything for a change from the drug-running he made his money from: that was what Sam said. Of the three of us Steppenwolf courted the worst kind of danger, smuggling in heavy stuff for the Vancouver families, running the checkpoints at airports from New Delhi to Bogota, from London to Mexico City.

After a tense trip, he'd hike to the beach, where he'd strip down and start running. He'd run for miles, Sam's crazy St. Bernard following him, though at a respectful distance. Later, he'd drift back, break out the beer, and downing a few bottles he'd say to me, always looking down at the sand: "Let's go out."

One day in March, when we were a couple of miles out, and tired, a big wave took us right out of the canoe. One minute everything was fine, then there was a sudden roll, a wild plunge, and I was swimming in cold water. I was scared pissless, choking, looking for the white blade of the beach.

Steppenwolf bumped against me; I felt his hand slap my shoulder. "Come on," he growled, and pushed off for the shore. The boat had drifted out of reach.

It was a bad moment. I could feel my blood pumping slow, as if the ice was forming in a knot in my chest—when it spread out and reached my fingertips I would stop swimming. Luckily, that point came just as my feet touched the rocky shelf near a jutting land spur. I came out of the water shivering, looking around desperately for Steppenwolf, who had vanished just ahead of me as I approached the shore.

I staggered up on the beach, blue-skinned and trembling, knowing I was going to die from the cold; nothing could help me; there was no time to get help.

Then I saw Steppenwolf running down from the woods with a big handful of earth. I was too numb in mind and body to figure it out, but the possibilities struck me dimly, and comically: was he going to bury me, or massage me back to life?

I watched as he slammed down his bundle. It wasn't a clod of earth but a mouldy canvas bag, and when it split open there were matches inside, several boxes, carefully wrapped in tinfoil. I felt myself steered and half dragged to the trees. "He's going to light a fire," I thought. "How wonderful—he's going to light a fire."

Later, I drank a lot of whiskey and told Sam about it. Steppenwolf wasn't much for stories, and besides, he had gone back out after the canoe. He was a careful guy, and I was glad he had those stashes all along that beach. It wasn't the only time they came in handy.

Once we went up north to pick up two new canoes. They'd been made by some half-breed friend of Sam's, who swore they'd stand up to any kind of sea weather. We were planning to do some real exploring, whale watching, up by Graham Island, and needed something better than what we could rip off from the local suppliers.

That trip was the longest time I had spent with Steppenwolf and he told me a few things about himself. His real name was Peter Winford but Sam and I were the only ones in those parts who knew it. He'd been born in New England—Maine, I think it was—and his father was a doctor who was living somewhere in Florida, slowly drinking himself to death. His mother—she had some vague Canadian connection—had died of cancer when he was about fifteen. I got the impression he was very wrapped up with her. Steppenwolf had gone to some Swiss school where he'd started selling drugs and acquired his nickname. He'd come west, like the rest of us, to get cured of a lot of early memories he couldn't quite handle. Not that on the beach or in the woods you ever forgot the past; it was just that you had space to explode in when it finally caught up with you.

We brought the canoes back, hid them, and decided to get ourselves some steak, booze and company at the local hangout. There was a little hotel we knew—The Paradise, they called it, but it was about what you'd expect of something northwest of Strathcona. In those days there were communes in every godforsaken place and girls with strange names to share your bed for a night, so even the sleaziest backwoods hotels were often crowded.

This one looked like a converted barn; it was huge and unpainted with awkward dormers jutting out everywhere upstairs. From one side a single-storied shed ran; it was set with big windows, so that at night you could look in and see the bar and the dancing.

We arrived toward sunset; there was a yard full of vans and a few jeeps, somebody's battered red sedan and a motorcycle with a sidecar on which a peace symbol had been outlined in bright silver paint.

The place was pretty full. Loggers and old-timers from the park sat talking to the flower children; a few short-haired tourists ate their steaks, but kept sniffing the air and shooting nervous glances in every direction, while a crowd of businessmen, already soused to the ears, sprawled out beside a pile of expensive fishing gear, nudging each other, pointing at the hippies, and bursting from time to time into heavy laughter.

Steppenwolf and I eased our way up to the bar. In those places, when you came in, everybody looked at you. It was an arena where some things were taken for granted but others might have had to be proved—and you always wanted to know what you were up against. I guess we attracted a bit of attention. I myself stand about six three, and my hair is white blond. It's true they used to call me Little Jim, but that was a joke. I was pretty edgy in those days, though hard to stir to a fight.

Steppenwolf, of course, was Steppenwolf, though with some of the rough bush look smoothed out of him. His black hair, though neatly cut, hung right down to his shoulders, and he was proud of it. He was wearing jeans and a very expensive buckskin jacket, and hunting boots he had bought on one of his trips to England. At his belt, though no one could see it, was the big jack-knife he always carried, and sometimes touched for luck.

Everything was quiet at first. We leaned across the bar, drank, and talked to Tarzan, the bartender, a U.S. marine in exile, and to Meg, who ran around the tables with huge pitchers of beer, joking with everyone, and at the same time keeping an eye on the drunks. We were working up an appetite, and also having a look around the place for women. I made a joke about this and Tarzan winked and pointed to a table where two ladies were listening to a guy do a Grateful Dead imitation on a guitar. I guess he was pretty stoned because he kept interrupting himself and the notes seemed to float away, though his body went on swaying to some imaginary music— perhaps he was finding it in the girls' eyes.

"That's Vanilla," said Tarzan, leaning his grizzled red face across my beer and speaking in a comically loud whisper.

I looked suspiciously down at my beer. "What's vanilla?" I wanted to know—people were always spiking your drinks with stuff in those days; I thought for a second it was some new kind of acid.

"The girl, buddy, the blonde over there with Deborah Down." He nudged and winked in the direction of the table. I took a closer look at Deborah Down, a slender blonde with wonderful cheekbones, happy blue eyes and a lovely mane trailing down to her bum, and I thought of all the jokes you could make about getting or not getting Deborah Down. After that, and after a couple of more swallows of beer, I realized I liked her very much and that she was looking at me as if she was interested.

"I know Vanilla from before," Steppenwolf was saying in his quiet voice. "She used to hang around Gastown with the Out-to-Lunch-Bunch. She told me she would meet me in The Magic Theatre one day. I never saw her there."

The Magic Theatre was a hippie hangout in Vancouver. Somebody explained to me once that the name had some connection with Hesse's character, Steppenwolf, the original.

Now I managed to pull away from Deborah Down long enough to take in Vanilla. She was spooky-beautiful all right, with trailing dark hair, a long full body, and deep set eyes. She made me think of Rebecca in the Classic Comic's *Ivanhoe*. But there was also something that glittered in her glance that I didn't want any part of. I wondered what

Steppenwolf would do.

"Let's go visit the ladies," he said.

The guitarist had floated away somewhere and we sat down at their table. This kind of thing had happened before. We were always drifting in from the bush and quickly finding ladies to remind us of what we'd missed. Steppenwolf, not saying much, but conveying a kind of subterranean excitement, had a way of stirring things up. We took it for granted that everything was possible, that there wouldn't be any claims in the morning. Once or twice we got crossed.

I remember a girl showed up once at our beach hideout, someone Steppenwolf had slept with two nights in a row—a beautiful woman with a strong character at that. It seemed she had intentions of camping with us for a while. Steppenwolf took her aside, and talked to her very quietly, very lovingly, it appeared. I watched from a distance and I could have sworn I saw a tender, regretful look on his face. I did see him gently caressing her, obviously reassuring her. She left very quickly, as if in a kind of trance. Later I asked Steppenwolf what he had said to her. I guess I envied and wanted to emulate his easy mastery. "I told her if she didn't leave I'd throw her in the sea," he said. "I told her if she ever came back I'd kill her."

Vanilla, unlike most of the curiously re-baptized ladies I met in those days, didn't go in for small-talk about sun signs and auras.

"I've got a bottle of unblended whiskey and a stash of the best Acapulco gold upstairs," she told us. "It's a very nice room, one with a good view and a very hard bed. Now you see this backpack? In here I've got a new bikini I want to try on. It's just too hot to wear jeans, you guys agree?"

At this point she leaned across her drink, and her whole body shivered, and I got the sense that, under the table, she and Steppenwolf were already making contact.

"I'd like to eat first," said Steppenwolf, straightening up under my glance.

"Do you think you need to?" Vanilla asked him.

I looked at Deborah Down and we laughed. Vanilla barely smiled at Steppenwolf; she tilted her head back, and closed her eyes; she seemed to be concentrating on something. Then she stood up so quickly that I jumped.

She was wearing jeans all right, and for all I knew they might have been too hot. Her yellow cotton top, half-unbuttoned, parted when she bent to get her bag. We all looked—she had a way of making everyone watch her.

"See you later," she said, almost indifferently, and moved away toward the stairs. There was a little chorus of appreciation from the businessmen as she swept past their table.

From behind the bar Tarzan was watching Steppenwolf. Deborah and I were watching him too. I was hoping he'd go after Vanilla pretty soon; I didn't mind talking about sun signs. He swallowed what was left of his beer, got up, and without looking at us said: "Think I'll take a walk."

I figured he might be going outside to cool off. Instead, he stopped at the bar, swallowed a whiskey, and bent over briefly to exchange a few words with Tarzan. Then, just as Deborah Down finally asked me if I might be a Pisces, I saw Steppenwolf, with a familiar gesture, smooth out his jacket where the knife hung, and without so much as a glance at our table, trek on up the old staircase to the second floor landing.

"I think my friend is going to pay a visit to your friend," I told Deborah, interrupting her analysis of my Piscean temperament.

"If he does he's got a problem," she said quickly. "She's timed it just right for trouble because that dumb hunk who just walked in the door and is heading for the bar—he's her husband."

I gave Deborah a glance and then turned slowly;
I thought she might be putting me on.

There was a guy right enough, a big guy with
smooth darkish skin, a close-cropped bullet head,
and brawny arms swinging down from his cut-out
T-shirt. He was wearing light-tinted sunglasses,
overalls and mean-looking half-laced boots, though
he walked in these so lightly they might have been
dancing shoes.

He crossed the room slowly. His glance touched
in turn the businessmen, Deborah, me, and the
empty chairs at our table, but the faint smile on his
face didn't alter. He kept swinging what looked like
a metal bracelet or a handcuff—actually, it was a
key-chain—while he stepped to the bar, ordered a
couple of quick beers, and downed them.

Then he turned, eyed us for a minute or two, and
walked slowly toward our table.

Deborah's boot came round and nudged my right
foot.

"Let me talk to him," she said.

She introduced us. "Cliff, Jim," she said and I
nodded. He mumbled something, flashed his white
teeth (they surprised me), and sat down.

Meg, the waitress, came over and I ordered a
round of drinks for us.

"Where's Vanilla?" Cliff asked, without any preliminaries.

"I think she probably went back to Jill's place," Deborah told him. "I'm not sure."

Cliff laughed. It was all on the surface, he didn't seem much amused. The key-chain flashed as he swung it just above the table.

"Nice girl, that Vanilla," I ventured. He turned to me, straightened up, and threw me a sour look. "You really think so?" he said quietly.

"Sure," I said, not making it sound congenial. "She belong to you?"

Cliff looked at me. Deborah's boot came against my foot. But I knew what I was doing. He wasn't big enough to kill me with his bare hands, and if I could get us thrown out of here, I might be able to stop something worse from happening upstairs. I knew from the way he had talked to me, from what I guessed, what kind of game Steppenwolf would play with that lady. He was no slow-fused lover. He and Vanilla were likely to have a roll in the bed, a couple of drinks and come up laughing. A little spasm of lust, like animals mating, cheap satisfaction. (In those days of sweet freedom, unless we were really stoned, none of us got very far into love-making.)

I knew if I could keep this son-of-a-bitch busy for

half an hour, Steppenwolf and I could walk away without getting into trouble. Actually, I was doing Cliff a favour. I took in what he had going for him and the conclusion was obvious: if it came to any kind of gutter-fight with Steppenwolf it wouldn't go well with this boy; Steppenwolf would just kill him.

"You know where she is?" Cliff asked me, leaning close and fixing me with his unsmiling, dark eyes. I could see his knuckles tighten around the beer-mug.

"I think she's at Jill's," Deborah repeated. Her imagination seemed to be failing her in the pinch.

"I'm talking to *him*," Cliff insisted, not looking at Deborah at all, but keeping his gaze fixed on me. I just laughed and stared him down. After a while he said "Shit!" drained the beer, got up and shoved at his chair. It fell over and he didn't bother to pick it up. Nobody else paid any attention. He turned and walked across to the bar.

"I told you not to fool with him," Deborah whispered, slapping fiercely at my sleeve with one of her ring-smothered hands. "I might've been able to get him over to Jill's, but now he'll ask around until he finds out where she is. You stay here and watch him, and I'll run upstairs and warn them. It's just the kind of mess Vanilla likes, but for sure somebody's going to get hurt. I hate all this violence you guys get into!"

"So do I," I confessed to her. She looked very pretty when she was angry—always a good sign. I shrugged my shoulders.

Over at the bar, Cliff was talking quietly with Tarzan, who kept shaking his head and looking baffled. He was very good at it, but it didn't look like Cliff was fooled.

Deborah got up and made as if she was heading for the ladies'. Cliff saw her and moved. I started to get up, but he let her go, swung past me, and stopped at a nearby table where a couple of young fishermen were getting smashed. He sat down with them, slapped one of them on the shoulder, and started talking them up in a low whisper. It looked like he knew them pretty well.

I saw what was happening and waited, and sure enough, as Cliff talked, one of them looked at me, smirked and looked away. They both began whispering and pointing across the room to where the stairs curved up to the second-floor landing.

I'd been holding my breath while Deborah was moving up that rickety curved stair; luckily Cliff had his back to it. She disappeared at the top just as Cliff began to look very grim, nodding his head as the men spoke, and then peering back over his shoulder. The light caught his face then, twisted into a contortion in which I read anger, pain, and that curious baffled look men often have when they learn their sweet ladies have betrayed them.

He stood up suddenly. The chair wobbled, but didn't go down, yet there was violence in the way he swelled his shoulders, in the way he swung that key-chain in his clenched fist.

He crossed the room without looking at me and started up the stairs.

I got up too, then suddenly someone was holding my elbow. Tarzan had come around the bar and shoved his face so close I could see the scar above his left eyebrow where they'd cut him for running away the first time from the Marines.

"No trouble, now, Jim. You know the rules here."

He held me by the sleeve but kept smiling. The guitarist who had disappeared had turned up again, on a bench in the corner. He had started playing "Tambourine Man," and the crowd began to sing along, a little raggedly at first, while I bent over with a few words for Tarzan.

"That guy Cliff, he's gone upstairs and he'll find my buddy with Vanilla. There's going to be trouble unless I get my ass up there in a hurry."

"If I let you go, do your thing and cool it. I don't want any bodies coming through the ceiling. If I hear anything, even a peep, you all get bounced. You got it?"

"Sure."

Tarzan let me go. He had the kind eyes of some father confessor, much too good for this world. Maybe that was why he had run off to the boondocks.

I got up the stairs in a hurry. The second-floor hall glowed faintly with a dim green light, but at the far end one of the doors had been flung open, making a bright patch on the scuffed wood. Voices came from there.

I hurried along and found a strange scene in the bare ugly room.

Vanilla, completely naked, sat on one of the high beds. (There were two of them, twinned—they looked like they'd been bought from a hospital). Deborah stood beside her, trying to get her friend to cover up with a shirt or some odd bit of underwear.

Cliff stood almost in front of them. I couldn't see his face. He wasn't moving or saying anything, just standing there.

Steppenwolf sat in a chair a few feet away. He had tipped it back and was balancing himself, resting his boots on the table, and spreading his arms out as if he were about to fly away. He looked exactly like Henry Fonda playing Wyatt Earp in the old John Ford movie, and I knew he was aware of the fact.

The room was anonymous. I saw a couple of other chairs, two big lamps, a table with a telephone and an empty water pitcher. The bedspreads and curtains were a sickly green.

It was no kind of setting and the light was very bright but even in that light Vanilla looked pretty sensational. Her dark hair fell down to her shoulders. She had large lovely breasts, wonderfully shaped legs—all the equipment, as we used to say— but what hit me hardest, what made me almost fall in love with her on sight was the unselfconscious innocence of her body. Of course she herself was no doubt anything but innocent, a real manipulator in fact. But at moment she carried herself so simply, so honestly, it seemed, and without a trace of coquettishness, that I almost believed in her simplicity, not to mention her good healthy animal instincts.

"It's getting crowded," she said, noticing me where I had planted myself in the doorway. She bent over to massage her ankles a little, as if she had just stepped out of a bath.

As she did so, Steppenwolf, who was sitting

behind her, stopped his balancing act. His chair bumped down.

Cliff swung his key-chain violently at his side, swore, and took a step toward the bed.

"Why don't all you guys get the hell out of here," Deborah said.

"Are you coming with me, or do I have to kill this bastard?" Cliff said, then swore again.

Steppenwolf stood up, his right hand playing around the belt where his knife was.

"I don't think your girl wants to go with you," Steppenwolf said. "We were just about to order some champagne when you came butting in here."

"This is my *wife*, you asshole."

"I don't think your *wife* is too keen on you," Steppenwolf said. His soft voice sounded confident. "I think she wants to stay with me for a little while."

"You son-of-a-bitch! Who the hell do you think you are, coming in here like this?"

"Vanilla invited me up here. I'm her guest."

"I think you all should clear out," Deborah said. She was very nervous and kept trying to cover Vanilla with bits of clothing.

"I think we ought to talk this over," I said. "I promised Tarzan there wouldn't be any trouble up here."

Steppenwolf winked at me. "There won't be any

trouble, Jim. You take this sweet guy downstairs and buy him a drink. Deborah too.... Unless she wants to stay here with us."

He spoke very quietly; there was no triumph in his voice, just a matter-of-fact confidence; he almost sounded indifferent.

"Fuck you," Cliff told him. "I'll cut your fucking balls off."

There was a silence and then Vanilla suddenly began to laugh. She wasn't laughing at Cliff (I think he would have killed her if she had been), but at the rest of us, at the wonderful scene she had created for us.

Steppenwolf moved toward Cliff, stopping just out of arm's reach in front of him; then he turned round, keeping Cliff on his left side, while his gaze took in Vanilla on the bed. I could see his Adam's apple move in his throat as he looked at her.

"Should I throw this creep out?" he asked her.

Vanilla looked at him. She closed her eyes as if she were pondering the question.

"I don't think so," she said in a bright voice. "I think I ought to invite him into my bed, don't you? After all, he's my husband."

We all looked at her, all three of us men. I thought she was playing with Cliff and I was ready to grab him before he went for her. Steppenwolf said: "Don't push it too far, Vanilla. The guy's upset."

"I'm not pushing it too far, at all," she said. "*You're* pushing it too far. I invited you up to show you my bikini. I didn't say you could ball me, did I? Cliff is my husband and I was just killing some time while I was waiting. Don't you remember, Peter? You just don't turn me on."

I was astounded; he had told her his real name. He took her seriously enough for that. It was unheard of. And now she had profaned it.

Cliff, who understood almost nothing, laughed. Steppenwolf didn't move. I could see he was reading her; he was trying to figure out how to deal with her.

"Don't make jokes like that," he said finally.

"I'm not joking," she said. "Get the fuck out of here, Peter, and go back to the woods—where you belong. Don't wait around for me to fall over you."

Cliff laughed again and moved toward the bed. Steppenwolf reached for his knife and Deborah cried out: "No!"

I grabbed my friend and held him while Cliff backed toward his wife, holding his fists down low.

Vanilla sat smiling, as if proud of herself. Deborah's hands were shaking and she looked at me and said: "Can we get out of here, please!"

Steppenwolf stopped resisting, but I felt the

weight of his body: he leaned on me. His hand hung at his belt. Vanilla was clinging to her husband.

Deborah said: "I hate these games."

"See you tomorrow," Vanilla said "Late tomorrow... Goodbye again, Peter."

She laughed. Her body looked more beautiful than ever as she pressed herself against Cliff's rough-cut shirt.

I started to pull Steppenwolf out of there. He didn't resist. Deborah leaned on me and we made a comical sight, I guess, stumbling into the hallway, like a strange hooked-together creature. The door slammed hard before we reached the stairway.

On the way down the stairs Deborah said: "She gets her kicks from this kind of thing. But Cliff is such a jerk."

Steppenwolf said nothing. He smiled quietly to himself, brushing off his buckskin jacket, touching his long hair with his fingertips.

"Would you guys like to buy me a drink?" Deborah asked, as we stood between the noisy bar and the darkness of the parking lot. But I saw Steppenwolf wasn't buying anything; hunched over, turned in on himself, he was already heading out into the night. I looked regretfully at the beautiful Deborah. She seemed to offer endless promise, comfort, and bliss without pain. They all did, in those days, I guess.

"Not tonight...." I said bravely, realizing there might never be another. "How about a telephone number? Have you got a telephone number?"

It took us a while to find a pen and paper, to get the number down, and for me to see if I could hold her long enough not to have to let her go.

I let her go; she turned and disappeared into the bar.

The parking lot was crowded now with vehicles, full of pickups, bikes and battered sedans, and I had some trouble finding our old Chevy truck.

There was no sign of Steppenwolf in the cab. I found him on the other side, sitting on his haunches, his big dark frame propped against the front tire. He was swinging his knife up and down, laughing quietly, plunging the blade again and again into the loose parking lot gravel.

"You okay?" I asked. "You wanta go back in?"

I knew he didn't but I was beginning to feel sad about passing up Deborah.

"Let's take off," he said. "I want to get out on the water. I want to go out in the canoe tonight."

I thought of the dark sea, the swinging waves, the cold spray on my cheeks. I thought of Steppenwolf saving me, building that fire on the beach.

"She's a bitch." I said. "Let's get the hell out of here. Get out on the water where we feel good."

Steppenwolf looked at me. Did he sense that I wanted to ask him why he'd told her his real name?

"It doesn't matter," he said. "Just a minute...."

He stood up, then raised his arms above his head. His knife blade flashed flash briefly in the darkness.

With his left hand he was holding his hair, that long thick hair he was so proud of. He held it steady, while with the blade of the knife he cut off bushy handfuls of it.

He blew thick bunches of hair off his fingertips, laughed, swung the knife and cut still more. The knife flashed around his ears and his forehead. After a while he stopped, as if catching his breath.

Inside the Hotel Paradise, the music was getting louder. Lights beamed through the porch windows. Somebody must have turned the strobe on, and soon there would be dancing. The dancing would go on through the night, and for all I knew, forever.

Steppenwolf slipped his long knife back into its sheath. He brushed his shoulders, where a few strands of hair still hung. He flung open the door of our truck, and shoved me toward the seat.

"Let's move on," he said, and walked slowly around to the other side.

At Approximately Three P.M....

The man is making peanut butter cookies. His wife comes into the kitchen. She's been reading Virginia Woolf and typing up her dreams. She stands there, on the other side of the round oak table, and begins to speak. He's aware of how beautiful the day is, winter sunlight flaring up suddenly through the pines, striking the snow to countless fine-points of crystal. Through the newly installed sunroom doors he can see everything—it's all just as they planned and already a lot brighter in the old stone house.

The woman begins to speak in a crumpled voice. Their child comes into the room with some blocks. He asks in his two-year-old way for his TV programs but it's far too early, only three o'clock. He drops the blocks and says something incomprehensible about the carpenter who's been working on the bathroom paneling but has just now gone off for material. The sunlight continues to pour itself out.

The woman is explaining to the man that she is nearly at the breaking point. They've lived together eleven years and she's always been miserable, she tells him. Her face is tight and her voice faint and edgy. She'll have to go away, she explains, to take some kind of rest cure, she is so unhappy. The man puts the final touch, the vanilla, into the cookie dough and begins to knead it and roll it out. He rolls the dough into small dollops and presses them out with a fork. She must do whatever she thinks right, he tells her in a mechanical voice.

The oven has been pre-heated to 375 degrees Fahrenheit. The child drops his blocks and asks for his dinosaur book. It's as if the pines are on fire now, the sunlight angling up from some deep place in the fields beyond, almost blinding.

The man begins to put the cookies into the oven, shoving the trays in together and checking the temperature. The child ransacks his low kitchen bookshelf and pulls out his book about trucks. Turning the pages, he calls out the name of each kind of truck, skipping the ones he can't remember.

He pays no attention to his parents. The woman comes around the table and stands in the sunlight. She's wearing a navy blue sweater and jeans and her hands move nervously in the sunlight.

The woman explains that she may be going to have a breakdown. She has no freedom and no life with him, it is hopeless. She feels flayed every day they are together. The child looks up at his parents and comes across the room and around the table. He sits on one of the table's lion-paw legs and begins to chatter away nonsensically.

The man tells the woman that she should discuss this with her analyst. He says she's probably just drinking too much coffee. Then he turns to check the first batch of cookies, noticing sunlit crumbs on the bare hardwood floor.

The woman loses control and begins to scream. The man is alarmed and tries to brush past her. She swings out at him with a closed fist and deals him a sharp blow on the back of the neck. The child grabs hold of his mother, whimpering loudly.

The man feels the pain ringing out in his shoulders and neck. It's a clear signal, and makes him aware of himself. He's very nervous and cannot stop laughing. He thinks he may have been laughing before, when he mentioned the analyst and the coffee. He points frantically to the child and asks her please to control herself.

The woman controls herself with an effort. Every expression squashed now from her face, she picks up the child and sits him up on the table. The sunlight makes a gold-haloed fringe around his fairy-tale locks.

The man realizes the cookies are burning. It seems he has only just put them in the oven, even so, they are burning. He opens the door quickly with the frayed old oven mitts and pulls out the smoking trays. The cookies are burnt black and at the same time soft. He touches one and it makes a brown smear on the mitt.

The woman lifts her son down and collapses into a chair. She stares straight ahead into the sunlight. The man carries the cookie trays to the sunroom door and slides it open. A chill breath touches him. He throws the cookies away into the snow. A black cat runs out from under the porch and begins to paw at the cookies. The man closes the door and turns to the woman, not touching her. The child runs to the glass panel to look at the cat. The cat begins to eat the cookies.

The man sees the carpenter's truck returning. It stops in the driveway and the carpenter gets out.

His breath is steamy in the air. He picks up his toolbox and some wood from the truck and comes to the door. The child turns away from the cat and runs to the door to greet the carpenter. The man opens the door.

The woman's head sinks slowly down on the table, as if she might be falling asleep. Her breathing is regular, solemn. The carpenter starts carrying his wood into the kitchen. The child plays with the wood.

The man sees that their Husky has come to chase away the cat and to eat what's left of the cookies. The dog rubs its silver-grey fur on the darkening snow. The man thinks of putting on a record to cheer things up, because he knows it will get dark very quickly now. Instead, he pours himself a small glass of brandy and goes into the other room to sit down before the fire. After a while the child comes to join him. It's time now for the child's programs and the man turns on the television.

The woman lies motionless, sprawling across the table. The carpenter does not go upstairs to finish the bathroom. He begins to work right there in the kitchen, sawing and banging and drilling as the sun sinks lower and lower and finally disappears. The man comes into the kitchen and turns on the lights.

He sees his own reflection in the sunroom windows. When the carpenter finishes his task the man helps him lift up the woman. They lay her gently down inside the coffin. Her eyes are closed now and her breathing has stopped altogether. They stand there for a moment looking at her. The man is trying to remember whom to call. In the other room, the child begins to laugh and sing.

The House

Mitch rolled gently against the stranger who occupied his bed. His left hand, fingers extended, followed the slope of her shoulders, down to the hard spine. Out of spidery shadows and unwelcome splashes of light he made up a room, an ordinary one of walls and windows, his bedroom, to which he surfaced, a diver from a pool of dreams.

Beside him, the woman stirred in her pink nightgown. "Aren't you going to answer that phone?" she asked, her back pressing irritably against him. He pulled himself together and crawled out of bed. As he reached for the receiver on the dresser, the mirror nailed him, gray-faced and forty, the corners of his mouth drooping in vague apprehension.

"*May I speak to Mr. Bradley?*" The woman's voice surprised him with its sharpness. Grudgingly, he identified himself—after all, it was only ten to eight.

"It's about your farm," she went on, "the stone house near Morrisburg? I was just talking to Mr. Lavergne about it—I got your number from him. You do own the house, don't you?"

His mind shot from panic to hopeful expectation. Could this be some kind of tax inquiry? Frantically, he tried to remember when he had last paid the rates. Possibly, though, she might be a buyer. If they could only sell the damned place, out of the blue, just like that... "My name is Julie Pilarcyck," the voice said. "I'm with Vanguard Productions, Toronto. We're doing the upcoming CBC series on the New Land. We were wondering if we could use your house for some on-location shooting."Mitch took a deep breath, blinked, and turned to his wife. She lay across a pillow yawning, blonde on white, her breasts coming out of the low-cut nightgown. The sight was a vague irritation. He stared round at the dishevelled room, at the pine furniture, the old lamps, the familiar woodcuts pencilled with light. All that stuff from the farm had never looked right in this high-rise, he thought. And now their old stone house filled with Lavergne's junk. How the hell could they do any shooting there?

"What is it?" his wife was asking him, starting to swing herself out of bed. "Who are you talking to?"

"Just a minute, please," he said to the woman at the other end. His wife stopped short, miffed at his tone.

"Not you," he explained, laying the receiver down on the dresser. He went to the window and drew back the heavy drapes. Glass doors revealed a little balcony with some scraggly plants and an exercise bicycle, and beyond, a shining array of buildings and rooftops, the Peace Tower set precisely in its familiar niche between two great hulking commercial giants.

He slid the door open, took a few deep breaths and turned back to the room. Rhona sat on the bed, rubbing her eyes and staring at the telephone.

"It's some woman from the CBC," he explained. "A company they've hired. They want to use the farm for a location. What do we do?"

"*For a location!*" Her incredulity echoed his own doubts. The farmhouse had been falling apart since they moved out two years ago. The old veranda had nearly collapsed, the roof leaked, the inside pipes had burst, the septic tank sieved effluent. After a year of dereliction—the year of their own marriage breakup—he had somehow persuaded the

Lavergnes to move in and do a few repairs. Though the rent they paid didn't come close to meeting the mortgage payments, it was better than nothing, even allowing for the purple paint, the electric blue wallpaper and the many other hideous touches the local family had doggedly insisted on adding to the decor.

Mitch shrugged his shoulders and moved over to pick up the phone. "I'll be right with you," he said. "I'm just consulting my wife." He put his hand on the mouthpiece and waited for a sign from Rhona.

"Well, why not?" she said, "It can't hurt the real estate value, can it?" She disappeared into the bathroom and Mitch tried to think if there were any important conditions he ought to insist on.

"You know it's an historic house," he told the woman on the line, realizing he had forgotten her name. "There aren't many like it in the area. Of course it's a little the worse for wear right now. We haven't started to fix it up yet, but I guess that doesn't bother you, or you wouldn't be calling."

He was aware that she had been talking to someone on the other end, and had missed what he said, but he didn't repeat it.

"We'd like to take down the television aerial and change the colour of the pump," she told him in her crisp way. "I presume that's all right with you."

"Um...Sure, I guess so. Just so long as you restore everything."That would be no problem, she assured him. The conversation seemed to be over. All he could think to ask her was when they'd be shooting.

"Probably tomorrow," she said. "Thank you very much. Good-bye."

He started to ask her to hold on, but the line clicked out and she was gone.

"Pushy bitch," he said, annoyed at himself for being so ineffectual. He paced up and down for a while, anxious to get a shower and a cup of coffee.

Rhona stuck her head out of the bathroom door. "Well, did she offer you any money?"

He was searching for a last cigarette in the crumpled pack in his trousers. He had tossed them in a corner when they had made love late last night. It had been very good again, almost like old times, he recognized, and he was pretty sure he knew why. It was because he had taken Catherine to a motel in the afternoon. It was always exciting for him to make love to his wife after he had been with his mistress. Curiously enough, the reverse didn't seem to work as well—he didn't know why.

"I didn't get any money," he said. "You didn't mention anything about money."

Rhona came out of the bathroom naked, dripping water, a towel wrapped carelessly around her middle.

"For an American you're certainly a terrible salesman," she said, sitting down before the mirror of her dressing table.

"Lay off, will you?" he snapped at her.

He wasn't sensitive about the American label; after all, he had been in the country fifteen years and felt as Canadian as anyone, and she knew very well that his job made a change of citizenship impractical. But the rap about his salesmanship hurt. It was true they were chronically short of money, but that was because they had the habit of splurging to cover every emotional crisis between them. His work as a lobbyist for a food multinational paid well enough, but they were very poor investors. The farm proved that: it was nothing but a white elephant, taken on so that she could try to recapture her past. The McAlisters, who had owned the farm for nearly two hundred years, and had sold out to them, reminded her of her own precious Moffit clan. What a bunch of prize yokels they were! And how bored she had been when she tried to settle down as she imagined her strapping aunts would, going to quilting bees and collecting old bits of pine furniture. Of course they did nothing of the sort, caught up as they were with Tupperware parties and snowmobile rallies. She had found the reality so tedious that she finally took a job in Ottawa, where before long she was having an affair with a particularly obnoxious senior management type. Over this their marriage had broken (more money!) but they had finally drifted back together, relieved, yet full of bitterness and new suspicions. It would take a long time to re-establish something like trust between them—if they ever did. And even though half-glad to be back with Rhona, Mitch had soon discovered in himself reservoirs of sheer anger he had hardly suspected. Out of spite, he hadn't told her about Catherine, whom he had decided to go on seeing, a fair insurance against his wife's possible vagaries, he decided.

He sat back with a cigarette and waited for Rhona to finish dressing.

When they had settled down over breakfast in the tiny sleek kitchen, she started in again on her favourite theme.

"I really wish we had done something with the farm," she told him sadly. "The house is so lovely, even if it is decrepit. No wonder they want to film there. Why don't you ask them for a free videotape?

After all, we ought to get something out of it."

"Do we have to go through all of this again," he protested. "You know you were bored as hell down there. You hated the place. Don't give me all that rubbish about your ancestors. You couldn't wait to get to town and find yourself—some distraction."

"I *worked* on that farm," she shot back. "You never took an interest. That's why I gave up. And don't insult me with your sarcasm."

The meal continued in a strained silence. After a while he got up and gathered his things together. "I'm going now," he told her, "if you want a damned videotape, you call her."

He lingered in their little entrance hall, wondering if it would be better if he cancelled out with Catherine so that he could take his wife to lunch. But that might be too complicated now—and besides, such efforts never seemed to work out quite right. In sheer frustration, and despite his best intentions, he slammed the door rather hard behind him.

In the elevator the muzak was playing as usual. There was nothing soothing about it. Halfway down he realized he had forgotten his door key. He always felt a little impotent without it and so reversed the car from the fifth floor to the eighteenth. He was about to bang on their door when he heard his wife's voice coming from inside. She was speaking on their hall telephone, and he paused as the conversation continued, inaudible. *It's taking her long enough to make the arrangements*, he thought, and then became aware that she was crying. Obviously, it wasn't the CBC lady on the other end. A little shocked, he decided he wouldn't interrupt; he could call her from the office and mention the keys. She must be talking to her mother, complaining to the old lady about him again.

Downstairs, in the main lobby, it suddenly struck him that her mother was at that moment in the middle of her annual summer cruise and that Rhona could hardly be phoning her. A sudden twist of suspicion riled him. He would have to talk to Catherine about this at lunch. She was always so good at helping him handle his wife.

2

Roy Lavergne raised the axe high and brought it down swiftly with a sharp clean blow. The wood jumped, split, and ricocheted against the shed boards. So there was another chip for the cook stove. He'd been cutting for half an hour now and there would be plenty of wood for the next week anyway. If only Lois would remember to keep the damper down a bit they wouldn't need so much. But it was no good reminding the woman; her head was always turned in the wrong direction.

Lavergne felt the sweat running across his face and brushed it away with the palm of his right hand, then spat in that palm for luck. That was what he needed, he thought, a change of luck. He stared gloomily at the three stumps of the fingers the company chainsaw had robbed him of five years back. From time to time, with a shudder, he remembered the pain, but the lawyers said that everything was going fine—his claim should be through within the year and that would make a big difference. Ten thousand dollars and he would be out of the woods for good. He could buy into a Morrisburg store, or pick up some land near Grantley and build himself a house. Once out of paying rent to those city sods, he would be home free.

He picked up the beer can from the log ledge and swigged it clean. Cheryl was supposed to be bringing another—where *was* that girl, he wondered—mooning around the barn, likely as not, playing with those mangy kittens. Just his luck to have three girls, four counting Lois who was more useless than his daughters—and as for Howard, well, by God, if he'd cut down on the pot and the booze he might amount to something. But of course like the rest of them he had nothing but big ideas— going to L.A. and all that. You couldn't talk sense to them with the television showing them where all the big money was and how to get it. If *he'd* ever let on to his father he was thinking of going to a place like L.A., he'd have had the hide beat off him. Old Dad didn't know L.A. from a hole in the wall—it was Montreal that was his pot o' gold—though he never did a thing but blow money there. And that was easy, seeing he had the lingo down and all that. It was a wonder how the old man could jaw away in both languages and make not a damn bit of sense in either.

"Cheryl!"

A flash of pink shot by the window, disappeared, and then reappeared in the shape of a ten-year old Lavergne girl with long golden curls. This daughter was just like his late Irish mother, he always thought, sensible, and not afraid of a little hard work.

"Cheryl, get me a beer, will you," Lavergne said, "and then go and help your mother make lunch. Aren't Marcy and Lynn back yet? Well, I didn't think they would be, at that. Laying around the beach all day...I want to see them when they get here, you make sure."

Lavergne strode out of the shed and into the blazing sunlight of the farmyard. He surveyed with strongly mixed feelings the improvements he was making everywhere: his new duck pond, dug without the approval of the owner; the horseshoe pit and brick barbecue; the pink flamingos and nigger boy ornaments on the lawn, and, best of all, the newly placed garden, transferred from the rock pile the owner had picked at, to the much more workable, well-manured soil by the barn. While all this gave him pleasure, it was also a source of deep irritation; he was doing it for a city sod who couldn't care less, and when he moved out, which the next rise in rent would force him to do, there would be never a thank-you and no way to carry much of it on to the next place. That was the trouble with renting, he told himself bitterly, you work your ass off for the owner and you're no further ahead when you leave. Besides which, you have to pay for the privilege.

He stood in the centre of the yard over the big trough of fresh water he had run for himself to keep the heat off in this bloody weather. Staring down, he saw with pleasure the reflection of his own sweating torso—the strong shoulders, big-muscled arms and the black-bearded chiselled face the town girls fancied. By God, sometimes he was sorry he was a tied-down family man. The pleasures were few and far between for someone like himself, what with Lois gone to fat and chocolates, and with no spark or spunk in her any more between the sheets. By God, he'd like to get his hands on that city lady, the Mrs. Owner, a fancy little tart she was, as he'd heard from Arnold more than once. How she used to go out in the barn and cry on that lucky bastard's shoulder about her husband neglecting her, letting such a one as Arnold take her clothes off and roll her around in the loft when he was supposed to be taking the hay off the fields for her old man. Some hay! She was obnoxious enough, on the face of it, to everybody—truly, she was one lady he'd rather rent than own any day.

Lavergne spat, and plunged his head and brawny shoulders into the water, splashing it up over his thick dark hair, damping his hair down, sputtering and loving the run of the water, not too warm, on his body.

Another shout to Cheryl that brought a nice fresh towel, and he was feeling much better and ready for lunch, and so he trudged on over to the big house, wondering when the veranda would fall down, and whether the owner would ever come up with the money for a new one. It was too bad, really; he himself could have built one that would last. There would be none of that tongue-and-groove nonsense on his to let the rot in, and the posts would be properly sunk and anchored, with some bright paint to cheer things up, lime green maybe. In the old days they didn't have much idea about convenience. They did what they could to get a roof over their heads, and to give them credit, the house was still standing, a big gray pile of stone, not much to look at, but pretty solid considering the McAlisters had put it up. From what he'd heard that family didn't have much going for it, but some of them at least had some notion of how to build a house, that was certain. Only no money to improve it, and least of all this city lad, who'd let the well go off and given the kids more than one sick night until he had called the Health Department in Cornwall to complain about it. Not to mention the rats that kept getting in—to see the potatoes dragged across the kitchen every night was enough to make you sick. And not a shred of insulation against the damned cold Why, the heating bill alone would have you in hock, if it wasn't for the wood stoves.

He shook his head, coming in under the sagging

veranda, only to be met by the light-footed Cheryl, breathless with a message that stopped him in his tracks and made him squirm a little.

"The Hydro! Asking for me!" he cringed away and took a good swig of the fresh beer, then said sourly to his daughter:

"Just tell them your mother's sick again (*after all, she sleeps so much she may as well be sick*, he thought) and your father's not here. Never say your father's here, girl...Tell them I'm out on a contract, that'll impress them. I'm out on a contract—in Ottawa."

He lingered, not following his daughter into the house. Somehow he didn't like to hear her repeat a lie. He knew Lois wouldn't answer the phone either, what with the Hydro threatening an immediate cut-off over the bill. Of course he would pay; he always did pay and they bloody well knew it. He had no money coming to him until the weekend though, and they'd just have to wait. Naturally, it was no good telling them that, and besides, it made a man feel small to apologize to those bastards.

Sensing his anger rise at the injustice of it all, he seized the rough wooden pump handle angled above the well a few feet from the kitchen door and swung it rapidly until the water gushed. He ran his rough hands in the cool water, rubbed them off on his jean shorts, picked up and finished the beer, then quickly entered the house.

The kitchen was dark and cool. Lavergne saw with relief that he daughter was off the phone.

"Everything all right?" he asked her, with some embarrassment.

"They said they would expect payment by Monday or they were afraid they would have to...discontinue the service." She repeated the message by rote, a little stiffly, and edged away, anxious to be out of her father's orbit.

He stood frowning over the white plastic Colonel Sanders bank that decorated an oilcloth shelf. The room was stuffy, shrouded by heavy drapes, so that they didn't have to look out at the land all the time.

"Okay. I guess you can get me another beer before you clear off. I see your mother didn't make lunch yet."

"Oh yes," the girl brightened. "There's ham salad sandwiches in the fridge. I helped make them. She's just lying down for a while. Can I get you a sandwich, Dad?"

Lavergne nodded resignedly and went on into the middle parlour. A big room with an old tin ceiling, which he had painted yellow, more windows covered with drapes, and the TV, a huge one, turned on without the sound. Lavergne flipped channels and found a quiz show he sometimes watched. Before settling back in his easy chair he switched on the big artificial fireplace he had bought at Sears the year before. They were after him, too, the bastards, to catch up on his payments, but even if he lost it in the end, he had gotten plenty of pleasure out of this fireplace. Other people might think it ridiculous to have the thing turned on, flickering and glowing away in the middle of the summer with the temperature as high as it was, but to Lavergne it made the place seem like home. Naturally, one of the McAlisters sometime back had closed up the original old fireplace in the front parlour. They had no sense of comfort whatever, that family.

Lavergne sank down at his ease in the chair, muttering and shaking his head. Cheryl arrived with a fresh beer and sandwiches.

"Turn up the volume a little, will you, sweetheart," he asked her, and she obliged, then scurried away through the kitchen and outside, slamming the door.

Lavergne began to eat, letting his stomach rumble in pleasure over the beer and the sandwiches. Light winked steadily from the plastic logs in the fireplace.

3

The small car jolted along the rutted country road, in and out of the scrub bush land and along the fallen fences of abandoned farms. Julie reached down and retrieved her leather briefcase from underneath the seat. It was very early and she was still a little sleepy, but Pete seemed to be enjoying himself quite a bit, if in a rather negative way.

"God's country," he murmured mockingly, swinging them sharply and none too smoothly away from a series of yawning potholes. "Looks like all the locals are on welfare. Or maybe they just don't go in for fresh paint in this neighbourhood. Did you ever see so much rusting tin? Maybe we should just wrap up shooting at the Village and leave it at that."

"Now you sound like Pollard," Julie told him scornfully. Fumbling in her briefcase of papers, she located a fresh new roadmap and began to unfold it in her lap. "Believe me, I know what I'm doing. We're going to find what we're looking for and Al Pollard's going to eat his words. It'll be the show of the series. You know my instincts are always right about these things."

Pete shrugged his shoulders. "Well, you're the boss. But if you're wrong Pollard's going to scream.

At least you have Mary on your side. I think she's getting bored with Upper Canada Village. No wonder; what a cutesy claustrophobic place! Jesus, I'll be glad to get back to Toronto."

"We'll be on our way as soon as I get the scenes I want," Julie reassured him. "Try left here...There should be a fishing pond nearby. Maybe we can ask someone about the farms in the area."

A big untidy brick farmhouse lay opposite, beyond a picket fence from which the paint had long ago peeled. They turned, catching a glimpse across thick shaggy fields of the inevitable horizon of gloomy cedars. A dog chained to a dead elm barked at them. After a while they came upon four or five shacks among a spew of litter: piles of old garbage, a few junked cars and a lawnmower without wheels lay around the shabby buildings.

Nearby, two little girls were fussing over an immense life-sized doll, which they had propped up against a shiny new blue snowmobile.

"How about a little on-location shooting here?" Pete suggested, looking really grim for the first time that morning.

"That's our next project," Julie shot back. "An exposé of rural poverty. Do you want to talk Pollard into it?"

He shrugged his shoulders. She wasn't serious, of course. But Julie was thinking how good it would be to be free of Pollard, to get out of his orbit, to escape from his narrow ideas of what projects the company should take on. The uneasy working relationship between them, their intermittent and ridiculous affair, were beginning to irritate her. She realized it most of all when she was away and this time she was determined to do something about it. She had cut short the shooting of this patriotic historical series at Upper Canada Village, bored with the useful but ultimately tedious museum atmosphere of the place, and was planning to find herself an old house where she could do something really unusual. Luckily, she had control of the shooting, and the star of the episode, Mary Leavis, was quite happy to give her idea a try. They only had one day to find the place, though, and one day to complete the work. It was a risk, but if things went well she could go back to Toronto with footage that Pollard couldn't possibly refuse. The credit would clearly be hers—she would make sure everyone heard about it—and she could leave Pollard for something better at last.

"Could that be the pond you're looking for?" Pete broke in on her thoughts. He nodded toward a slate dark slash of water set among some recently planted trees and surrounded by a new-looking snake fence. Off to one side, there were a couple of wooden privies, a few heavy, chained-down picnic tables, but no sign of anyone. They pulled into the parking lot and got out, Julie carrying her map, which she spread out on a large stone that lay across the grass margin near the pond.

The early morning air was very light and clear, exhilarating in fact, and Pete inhaled deeply and stretched toward the sky in sheer pleasure. As she crouched by the stone, Julie was aware that he was looking at her legs, at the way she moved, and she rather enjoyed that. She had decided at the beginning of the assignment that she wouldn't sleep with Pete because he didn't attract her very deeply, but she might change her mind quite soon, she realized. She was bored, and though he was supposed to be happily married, she could tell it was a facade from the way he talked about his wife. As he picked up some pebbles and began skimming them across the pond, she watched his body moving lightly in the sunlight. In the distance she could hear a tractor labouring and groaning.

Pete climbed up on a huge outcropping of bare rock and looked in all directions, his hands cupped over his eyes to shade them from the glare. She began to concentrate on the map.

"Why don't we ask the farmer?" Pete shouted at her. He pointed on down the road in the direction they had been heading. "The fellow on the tractor, I mean."

"In a minute."

She thought she had pinpointed their present location on the map. From what they had told her at the Village, and from where she guessed they were, they might in fact be very close to the house she was looking for.

They got back into the car, drove rather slowly for less than a mile and found the tractor. It was a very battered peeling red machine run by a tiny delicate old man wearing blue overalls and a work cap. He was cutting the grass around the edges of a cemetery of something less than thirty gravestones. They got out and waited for him to bring his tractor around the margin but when he came full circle he didn't stop, only nodded slightly and roared past them, intent on his cutting.

"What do we do, lie down in front of the machine?" Pete asked, but Julie was already probing among the cracked and blistered tombstones, noticing how they had bleached white with age, like fossils.

Surely they could do a scene here too, she thought: it beat the Village any day. If she could shake Pete out of his preconceived notions on how to shoot it, things might work out very well.

He wandered away to try to stop the tractor, while she began reading the inscriptions: *Eliza Gallinger, died January 28, 1851, 21 years 9 months and 18 days. Gone to Rest; In Memory of John Wallace, died April 24, 1837....* Then suddenly a whole row of McAlisters, a name which sounded only vaguely familiar until she realized it was the name of the family that had built the house they were looking for. Just then the tractor quietened and Pete shouted and waved her over.

"He says the McAlister house is just down the road," he explained as she stepped out of the row of tombstones to where the tractor idled by the fence. From the other side a few cows eyed them, tails swishing amiably as they grazed.

"If ye're looking for Charlie McAlister, mind, you won't find him there," the old man was saying, nodding in greeting to Julie as she approached. "He moved to Morrisburg a while ago. Hated the farm, he did. Stopped farming and put the place up for sale the day his mother died. 'Twas the old lady that kept him there. Charlie had no stomach for it at all."

The old man leaned over from his seat and spat delicately away from his listeners. "There's more than one McAlister buried in this place, too. It was a McAlister first gave this land for the cemetery. Would you be related to the family then?"

"No," Julie said. "We're from Toronto. We're making a television show here. We'd heard the house might be a good place to do some filming, so we thought we'd take a look."

The old man's very blue eyes widened. "Television? Well, I never thought there'd be any television-making here. What show is it then? The missus and I'll be keen on seeing that."

Julie told him the name of the show. "It'll be on CBC," she explained, "but not for a little while. Next fall, probably. You can watch for it then. Who owns the McAlister house now, by the way? It's not a derelict, is it?"

"You mean left to fall down? Oh no. There was some fella from Ottawa had it and may still. But there's another fella lives there now by the name of Lavergne. Big family he has, and works in lumber—when he works. Not a bad fella that, but a little flighty. That's who you'll be finding there now, if he's awake."

"We're very much obliged to you for this

information," Pete told him. "Come along and watch the filming if you feel like it. It'll be later today or tomorrow probably. Don't bring too many of your friends, though."

The old man, very amused at the thought, cackled a little, and set his cap back rather jauntily on his head. He explained to them how they could get to the McAlister house. As they walked back to the car, Julie said. "I certainly hope he *doesn't* bring his friends." Behind them, the tractor roared and moved. They drove away and picked up the fork at the crossroads the old man had mentioned. There was a long five minutes as the road wound its way through mostly deserted countryside. Then, after sweeping a wide curve between two very swampy patches of land, they entered a long flat stretch, with several overgrown fields spread out on both sides of the road. On the right, about a hundred yards distant, they could see the house. Pete whistled softly, pulling the car off the road onto the shoulder when they reached the nearest field. They sat there for a minute and then looked at each other.

"Well," Pete beamed at her, "it looks like you've found your house. A bit seedy at the edges, but just right for what we have in mind. I bet the inside is filled with antiques, too."

Julie was already half out of the car. She walked quickly along the road toward the old house, keenly measuring the place as she approached. Yes, it was a stone house, and without too much gimcrack. True, it wasn't one of your closely manicured stone gems, but that was all to the good; they looked far too elegant, not the effect that was required at all. Of course the lawn ornaments were terrible, but they could shoot around those. But the old half-rotten veranda looked just right. Mary would enjoy doing the death scene there. Julie was sure now that the show was going to come out well. Luck was with her, there was every chance to bring this off exactly as she wanted. She smiled, imagining herself quite free of Al Pollard, moving on to something much better, perhaps enjoying a little fling with Pete before taking on a new job.

As she marched ahead, her excitement growing as she approached the house, she came in sight of a dark-bearded, burly man standing at one end of the porch and calmly watching her as he urinated onto the driveway.

4

John McAlister walked out of the deep woods that closely bordered his land and stopped for a minute to gaze across the wide fields of wheat at his fine new house. They were calling him now, Margery and his brother Malcolm, their voices rising out of the lively murmur of the relatives and neighbours who had gathered to celebrate the completion of the newest and most splendid house in the whole of Osnabruck township.

It was midday, the sun was high, the grain swayed gently in the light breeze.

This day, as John thought, was a special one, just as the year had been special, what with putting the new house up in place of the old wooden structure his grandfather, Hugh, had built and later held against both Indians and Yankee marauders. Slowly, the land had been cleared, then followed good harvests and bad, and a gradual accumulation of things that made life easier. The fruit trees his grandfather had planted, many of them, still bore rich produce, the maple bush yielded well, the cellar was stocked year by year. The old flax-made linens and homespun wools were giving way now to store-bought clothes, and the wooden bowls and spoons had been turned over to the use of the children. If all went well with the next few harvests there was even hope of getting a new Massey reaper, which, some said, could cut as many as twelve acres a day. Then life would be easy indeed and a man would scarce know what to with himself, if it wasn't for clearing new land, building and repairing, hunting and curing the hides.

Stepping along the hedgerows, McAlister could hear the voices of his children, Penelope and little Hugh, who were more than excited about the bigness of the house, so like a castle it was, for they had heard of such things from their Uncle Malcolm. It had been important for John to get away from the noise and fuss and the women's chatter to go into the woods for a brief spell of prayer before the feast. He liked sometimes to remember his father, who had died of a Yankee bullet at Crysler's Farm, to give thanks in private for all the good things that had come to the family since that tragedy, and despite the death of Margery's first two. They had hauled all the stone for the house from these very fields, and no horse or man had suffered, saving their neighbour, Richard Anderson, who had fallen under the wheels of the wagon, but he was walking again now and would be all right, the doctor said, by next spring.

As he approached his new house, McAlister felt the pride growing in him, seeing the fine clean stone rising out of the fields, the shining roof angled above the apple trees, a full storey and a half high. Everything was a harmony, he thought, even down to the tiny shell markings they had noticed on some of the big blocks the horses had dragged from the earth. Such markings, the Reverend Urquhart had said, had been imprinted by God on the stones in the very first days of creation. John McAlister thought with deep satisfaction how fortunate he was in having God's mark stamped on the very face of his house. This, he knew, was at last a true home for his children and their children, a house built to endure as long men lived in this country and worked in the fields.

His heart overflowing with joy, he stepped out of the farm path, and walked across the yard to join his family.

Visiting Mother

When I was a little girl, I didn't really know my mother. She was away, they told me, in the hospital; she was very sick. Mostly, I knew her photographs. Those I stuck in a big album, or in the fairy tale books my grandmother was always buying for me. Now and then I'd take the pictures out and sit for a long time trying to discover just what she looked like.

It's not that she had one of those nondescript faces that fade into the background before you can take them in. No, she would jump straight out at you, with her forties curls and lipstick, and her short-skirted baggy dresses, smartened with frills or little bunches of artificial flowers and berries. In close-up you could see she had a classic, almost an old-fashioned movie star face, with high cheekbones and dimples, strong white teeth, deep-set blue eyes and that perfect fair skin that always photographs well.

But that was only the start of it: for whenever I looked hard at those photographs—closing my bedroom door in case my grandmother would accuse me of mooning around—I could see that my mother, in almost all of them, had a smiling "come on" kind of look, as if she were about to say, "Well, why don't we go dancing?", or, "Let's take a drive and just fool around!" I couldn't express it then, but I guess I always sensed there was a streak of giddiness in her, innocent really, but a bit unsettling, as if she wanted to sprint away into a world of picnics and pink lemonade, where you could kick your shoes off and not mind the holes in your nylons or those bits of damp straw all tangled up in your mussed hair.

I lived mostly with my grandmother, at first in an old brick house downtown, then in the suburbs. My father seldom came around. He was so obviously out of place among the chintz-covered chairs, the delicate end tables, the Wedgwood, and the antique lace tablecloths. When my mother, at age nineteen, ran over and killed a poor drunken man, and it turned out the car insurance had expired, a great deal of my grandparents' money was spent in settling things. My father, her boyfriend at the time, was horrified. He was afraid that he'd be liable for the money.

Dad had never been particularly interested in Agnes, but he had appeared one day, fresh from the war, good-looking, compact and tough, and above all full of energy—very Irish with his red hair and his gab—and for a while my grandfather took him over, swept him up into the golfing set, introduced him to garden parties and martinis, and to his Bell Telephone cronies at the club.

It might have worked, I guess; Dad just might have been converted to all that, if things had gone right with my mother. He had been lured from a scrub farm in eastern Ontario straight into the worst of the war, coming back wounded, and like the other men who had fought in Normandy and the Ardennes, with a fierce appetite for the good things he'd hardly known before. Trading stories about trout fishing and chip shots with those bankers and insurance salesmen at the Royal Ottawa Golf Club, and being offered a house and a start in business, must have seemed something like a dream to him.

In the end, though, my mother did him in. There

had been a few signs beforehand, but after I was born, things went sadly askew between my parents.

Mother started to do weird things in the kitchen: she left the oven on all the time, scooped jello over the spaghetti, shouted crazy things out the window at the mailman. One day the phone rang: it was a wrong number and someone asked for Elizabeth. "Elizabeth only comes on Wednesdays," my mother told them. She began talking to the voices that she heard around her and inside her. "She's just a little strange, Jack," Granny assured my father, "but there's really nothing wrong with her at all." Never, not even at the end, when she must have admitted it to herself, would Granny acknowledge Mother's mental illness.

It was a big family gathering, held one summer weekend when I was about six, that finished father. He had taken my mother down—for only the first or second time in all those years—to meet his country relatives. The two sides of the family didn't get on at all. My other grandfather had two wives in succession and nine children, not carefully spaced, and lived in a homely frame house on a farm about thirty miles south of Ottawa. On holidays the whole clan got together—the Craigs, the Conors, and the McKelveys—Orange Irish who had settled long ago in those parts and never made it to the city and the sophisticated life. While other families dissolved around them, they hung together, sharing gluttonous feasts, consuming sides of beef and huge overdone turkeys, piles of boiled and sweet potatoes, and lots of bread and butter, with heaps of homemade pickles and relish on the side. They drank gallons of milk and coffee and tea, all except my grandfather Conor, who regularly sneaked away to the barn with a few of the other men to finish one or two bottles of rye. The women—those stout, close-cropped women with their masculine ways— baked dozens of pies, and after the meal they stood telling harmless off-colour jokes, as they scrubbed and wiped endless piles of soiled dishes, nearly bursting the walls of the kitchen with their raucous laughter.

In a way, I was responsible for the trouble. I loved watching the animals—horses, pigs and calves and even a goat—and that day I must have seen something, for it occurred to me to wonder why nobody seemed to mind that they didn't wear any clothes. I asked my mother about it, and she explained that since the animals couldn't talk, there was no chance of gossip, so it didn't matter what they did. But I remember, right after she told me this, in her slow dreamy voice, a kind of strange light came into her eyes, and she got up and wandered away, out toward the barn and the sheds.

It was a hot day and I went off with my cousins to pull the coke bottles out of the creek, when all of a sudden I heard the most awful shouts, followed by a terrible uproar, all the relatives bellowing and screaming at each other between the barn and the house.

I ran up from the hollow with the other kids, and the first thing I saw was my Grandfather Conor, a tall gangly man with a white beard, staggering across the yard, a half-empty bottle of whiskey in one hand. He was followed by several of my uncles and older cousins, some clearly smirking, while opposite there hung a crowd of women, all massed together, waving their arms and shrieking, their bodies twitching with a ferocious, half-suppressed laughter.

Something in me panicked when I saw and heard the fuss: I guess I had experienced a few things already. Then I caught sight of my mother and I remember wanting to run away, but my legs wouldn't take me anywhere.

Agnes was dancing, stark naked, on a thin, sun-shrivelled patch of grass, turning her hips and shaking her breasts, then raising her arms up to heaven, looking for all the world like a parody slave girl right out of some foolish de Mille epic, yet at the same time moving with a kind of dignity and freedom and seriousness, that made the whole performance truly shocking.

Of course, as I stood there, at first gaping, then quickly hiding my face in my hands, I was thinking of myself, of my own feelings. When I was older, and thought of it again, the humiliation and terror came back, but I remembered my mother, how she refused to stop dancing, even when my father came with a raincoat to cover her. She wouldn't leave her trance of real happiness, but sashayed across the yard in the raincoat, pulling it playfully across her body, as if it were all part of the act.

As for the relatives—a hush fell over the whole gathering. They all simply froze, as if a spell had been spoken from the shadows of the old barn. Finally, one of my aunts put her hand over her mouth to cover her smirk and giggled very loudly. The kids, shuffling around me, snickered and pointed at mother. Then my grandfather bellowed out: "*Jee-sus Christ!*" And everybody laughed like hell. When the laughter buzzed around the yard I thought I could hear the animals—grandpa's bulls and stallions—snarling and stamping in the back fields.

Everything dissolved in that hateful summer light, in the foul heat. I felt my body go rigid; I couldn't breathe or speak. When Aunt Lena came over and put her arms around me, I thought I would vomit. Instead, I burst into tears.

They led me away to a stuffy little bedroom, and brought me an aspirin and some tea, but I couldn't stop crying.

I never wanted to see my mother again.

2

I didn't have to worry. They took her away and shut her up again in the Brockville psychiatric hospital, a grim, silent place overlooking a wide but vapid expanse of the murky St. Lawrence River.

My grandmother had Agnes removed just long enough to have the hysterectomy done. My mother was about thirty-five then. When Father found out, he went flailing around, unleashing his anger in that wild, helpless way that was becoming typical of him. To get even, he had Agnes released from custody. That was how she came to live with my grandmother and me for a few years in the Ottawa suburbs.

I guess they figured it was all right for her to go home, that she was functional. But she had grown terribly fat, and her face had lost all its shape. Something had happened to her teeth; and they had clipped and permed her hair, colouring it a glossy false black, so that it looked like a wig. Her eyes, though, were as mild as ever, even if there was no fun in them now.

She settled down and went through all the motions of being a housewife, though things came out a little strange: the clothes stuffed into the dryer with soap in them, lemon meringue pies made with Kool-Aid, the hardwood kitchen floor carefully scrubbed and then fresh-painted green.

And sometimes I would be walking home with my girlfriends and we would meet her, as she trudged along to the supermarket, wearing even in summer a tattered fur coat and an old pair of stockings rolled halfway up her legs. Never once, on those occasions, did she look at me, and I always tried to pretend that she didn't exist.

Once my boyfriend's mother came to our house to pick me up. It was a beautiful summer day, and our visitor sat in her car, waiting patiently in our driveway. I got in beside her, but she didn't move. I could see her pouty lips quiver, and her fingers clutching hard at the wheel. Then she said softly, in that polite, silly way she had: "Jennifer, what on earth is your mother doing over there?"

I realized then that she had never quite understood the situation at our house. I took a deep breath and looked into the shadows of the garage.

My mother was sitting in a big fancy rocking chair, dressed in her fur coat, and wearing a hat she must have borrowed from my grandmother's collection, a Gigi straw hat with long trails of blue ribbon. She had no shoes and socks on and I could see her toes wriggle as she rocked, back and forth, the rhythm never varying. Piled up high all around her, were green plastic bags stuffed with garbage.

3

When I was a senior in high school my grandmother, in a drunken stupor, fell down the basement stairs. She was taken to the hospital and they had to amputate her legs.

I went to see her. I could tell that she didn't want to live any more. "Don't worry about anything," she told me. "I've made arrangements for your mother."

Agnes was back in the psychiatric hospital, and I drove down for a visit. The place seemed pleasant enough at first, a restful old brick building, surrounded by smooth lawns and curving driveways; in sight were prosperous houses and mansions—all quite reassuring.

Even I was reassured, for I had never been there before, not into the wards, that is. So when the nurse appeared, carelessly jingling her keys, I simply smiled.

I was led by the nurse down a long corridor that was spotless and shining, through white double doors, as if we were entering a kitchen. Then suddenly everything was dimly lighted, and we were face to face with what looked like a steel vault, grim and somehow implausible, set in the bare wall.

Quickly, the nurse selected a key and before we could exchange a word, she had swung the door open. Inside, someone was howling. The sound of it made me feel naked and vulnerable.

We came into another corridor: off to the left was a waiting room: bare, smoke-filled, its battered chairs and tables piled high with old magazines. The lime green walls were smudged and dirty. The main ward lay dimly ahead; the howling came from there.

The nurse hesitated; my mother walked out of the waiting room. She was dressed in a cheap white hospital gown. Without looking at us she started to speak. Her lips, curled and swollen, from the shock treatments, emitted a few sounds. Her hair was quite gray now, I noticed.

"Would you like to see my bed?" I believe she asked me.

The nurse stepped briskly toward the ward. She had locked the door behind us. I stood there frozen; a feeling of panic came over me. I took Agnes' arm and struggled along and we entered a large room without windows.

All around, the beds stood up like tiny crumpled islands. In one or two places women clung to these beds and screamed. They slumped across them or lay back, just howling. I don't know why it was the women who screamed. There were a few men, too, but they were silent.

Our nurse went off to talk to another nurse in one of the little rooms adjoining. Mother led me, without getting lost, to her bed: she knew the way.

"So this is where you hang out," I said, putting one arm around her shoulder. It was the best I could do, under the circumstances. I couldn't think of more, though I wanted to. The screams kept preventing me.

I don't remember anything else. After a while the nurse led me back through the steel door. In the big public waiting room other visitors sat fidgeting, waiting their turn.

Not long after this, my grandmother died.

I didn't want to go to university, so I got a job and moved to the country, alone. I could see my mother there sometimes, and there wouldn't be any questions. None of my father's family kept in touch.

It was an old stone farmhouse, with big rooms that flowed into each other, and my mother would pace the whole length of it, either upstairs or down, then wheel around and walk back, not ever stopping unless you forced her to. Sometimes I would try to distract her. I would sit her down and question her, as if I wanted to reassure myself about something. I made her answer what seemed simple questions.

"Where were you born?" I would ask her. "What's the name of the nearest town?" "What country is this?" "Which way is north?" "Do you remember your mother?"

I would get frustrated when she forgot, which she always did, but Agnes remained calm, staring out at me with that mild-eyed calf look that the drugs, perhaps, had given her. Once or twice, though, when she was just stupidly gazing at me, I could have sworn I saw a flicker of humour pass through her eyes.

My mother was over forty then, and it occurred to me that I knew nothing whatever about her, except for a few meaningless details, the kind of thing I had tried so hard to get her to memorize. During those visits a strange kind of stop-frame would happen: there were moments in which I would look hard, or touch her, hugging her close to me, or watching her, I'd think, *yes, this is my mother—but who*? Then the moment would pass and she was gone.

And she watched me too. I remember one afternoon in the country I had two visitors, a friend from work who insisted on bringing a guy she was seeing. I got through it all right, but at one point, after some boozing up, we were all frolicking on a hammock, when suddenly the rope strands parted and we fell, very hard, on the hard earth.

I got a bad jolt; and the others were in pain. I looked up and saw my mother sitting there on the veranda, watching us closely. She stared at us, the way a cat does, taking everything in without involvement, without emotion, just watching, the way God watches.

My father died shortly after that. It took about a year; it was painful, though. He didn't get over to see mother. Luckily, by this time, Granny's money had set Agnes up in a nice little nursing home in the country.

It was called the Sweet Brier Residence, and was located in a small tourist town some miles south of the city. I visited her there.

The place was rather nondescript, just one long low building, almost like a primary school, but with gardens surrounding it, and the woods crowding up on all sides. I remember one visit in late spring or early summer. Nearly everything was in bloom: there were beautiful pink roses growing along the curved walkway that led to the check-in point.

I fetched my mother from her pleasant room. Thanks to the drugs, she was able to talk now, a little, though mostly in response to questions. I had decided to take her out for a drive, to show her the river, to let her walk in the sunlight.

I thought I was at my best that day. My mother, who had recently been operated on, looked thin, almost frail, but her hair was soft and delicately curled; she was wearing a small-print Laura Ashley dress I had just bought for her.

I took her on my arm and led her out. "Why, Mum, you look wonderful," I said, really enjoying her. "You look like a beauty queen."

She smiled then, and as we walked along the path, she bent to touch a flower. "I'm just a rose," she said quietly, "a rose that weeps sometimes."

I took her free hand and squeezed her fingers.

4

A few weeks later she became seriously ill. They had to move her to a hospital.

My father used to say that probably Agnes would outlast us all, that my grandchildren would be dragged off to see her, still visiting Mother. I used to think of that sometimes, elaborating on it in my mind, imagining her being moved from place to place, from nursing home to nursing home, getting only so old and then stopping. Why, maybe she would even live forever.

The reality is more like this. It's a bright spring day in the country. The farm looks wonderful. For once I'm glad I live there, even though, now that mother's not with me, there's really not much point. Then the telephone rings and the hospital passes along the message: my mother has died in her bed overnight. Heart failure, apparently.

I walk out on the veranda, shaken helpless with

sorrow. I realize how much I hate them all—my grandmother, my father, and Agnes too, whom I had visited so many times but never knew.

I run through the yard, through my little garden, my boots kicking at the overripe, half-rotten tomato plants. I run toward the barn, the big empty barn, with the fallen boards, the sagging roof. I see the fields stretching away, corn stalks, shaved and mangled, the dull earth.

The latch of the door is stuck (in all these years I had never fixed it), but I swing the wood back on its hinges and somehow get into the barn. It's deserted, of course, no life there—just rotting straw, rats, and the smell of the past.

Now I can't control myself. I begin to cry, maybe to scream. Everything is so empty, everything is rotten. I pull all my clothes off and lie down in a pile of straw.

"*Mother!*" I call out to the silence.

Then I get up and grope forward, to one of the stalls, to a stanchion. Curved metal, old leather, shaped like some instrument of torture. The roof high above, and a flutter of pigeons, deep shadows, the emptiness.

I push my head between the narrowest bars of the stanchion. I scream and since it feels better, I keep on screaming.

I walk slowly back to the house. Luckily, I have some tranquilizers. At last the numbness sets in—for a short while.

5

Mother is buried in the plot Granny purchased for her long ago, in the middle of the city, while my father lies miles off, in an old country cemetery. Barely two years have passed since her death. I've never visited either place.

After my father died, I had some dreams about him, strange ones, in which he was experiencing new things, and I was helping him along. With Mother it's been different—no such special dreams and mostly just a blank when I think of her. Long ago I did have an important dream about her, though; I couldn't have been more than seven or eight at the time. Still, I remember it very clearly, as I do all my dreams.

In the dream she had been shrunk down, like Alice in the story, and I was much bigger than she was. So I was able to catch her and get her shut up in a clear plastic bag. She kept struggling and thrashing around in that bag: she was desperate to get out.

Well, I wasn't cruel; I wanted to let her out, I wanted it so badly, but in the dream I didn't, I couldn't, for a very good reason. I was afraid.

Granny used to tell me that on the way home from the hospital with me, Agnes had some kind of fit and let me fly out of her arms; she didn't really drop me; she just let me fly free. Well now I'm as far away from her as she could ever have wished, but have I ever been free? I've tried so hard to find her. I've searched all my memories, really pursued her. All those years I thought that one day, in one shining unexpected moment, I would suddenly know her, that we would acknowledge each other in some final, perfect way. Too bad it didn't happen— not even once—and now she's gone forever, and I've run out of places to look.

Famine

Before their fight the Craig brothers had lived together for nearly twenty years on the desolate scrub farm just beyond Hayley's pastures. It was Garnett's farm really—he was the eldest, and after their father's death he had moved back to those rocky seventy five acres with his new wife while Walter was still in the service.

His wife was an old-fashioned woman, tall and straight and beautiful, and she hadn't minded the lack of comforts—the worn linoleum, the wood-stove, the dirt, and the well drying up too often, but when he began to beat her, she went sullen. How it had all happened, he could never figure out exactly, or even remember. But sometimes pictures of her came back to him and he saw her crouched in the corner of their old bedroom, her white fingers clutching tight at her shift as she wept, refusing to let him touch her. Then he had found himself striking at her, as if some anger pushing up from his belly had exploded in his clumsy hands.

After six months, her father came and took her away, warning him not to try to get her back. The old man was a tyrant, known to be quick with his shotgun, and Garnett did nothing, not even going to town any more, for fear of meeting her or her relatives. He drove ten miles out of the way to get his supplies in Crawford, and switched to the church there too, or stayed home on Sundays and read out loud the great bound Bible he had inherited from his mother, who had died in childbirth with Walter.

At last Walter came back from the war, with an idea of living on the land. There was a steel plate in the side of his head from one of the last battles with the Germans, but he had money and fair health. He had been in the hospital a long time, but they had finally passed him out, even though he complained sometimes of a rushing in his ears, like the sound of water he said, swishing endlessly in some big trough.

He found Garnett scraping along on a narrow

margin. The tractor was old and there had been no replacement for the disc harrow that had been banged out of kilter on all those hidden stones; the tin on the barn roof was rusting badly and there were leaks everywhere rotting out the old beams. The crude pump that delivered water to the barn was barely functioning. Several fields were weeding up, and at the back corner the swamp had crept across the overgrown road, washing ancient daubs of cardboard and indestructible plastic from the farm dump across the old furrows.

Garnett had thinned down, it seemed to Walter, his face set hollow, his glance bending away too often from the matter at hand. He said less than ever and shrugged his shoulders more, sliding through the house, murmuring to himself whenever the door slammed, or an animal stirred in the night, or the wind caught the edge of a loose board. He had been almost a young man when Walter went away; now he was gray-faced and old, with slouching shoulders and a hopeless air, except when he read the Bible: then his voice picked up, rising from his sunken chest to fill the disheveled rooms with the strange music of prophecy or poetry.

When Garnett looked at Walter, on the other hand, he saw a young man who had gone rigid in a waking sleep, from which would sometimes burst with confident, impractical plans. Walter was possibly a little too fat; in learning something about the world he had lost his ambition. He hung back as much as he plunged forward, smiling to himself, but never talking about the past. He threw all the money he had into the farm almost as if he were in a poker game making a desperate bet on a bad hand.

Slowly, however, the house got fixed up. The weathered clapboard was covered with white siding; the old woodstove was hauled away and a furnace installed. Plywood paneling spread gradually through the rooms like a reassuring skin. They bought a new tractor, repaired the barn roofs, replaced the equipment, and bought some stock. A sit-down mower appeared, a snow-blower, new saws, and other tools. A lawn was planted and cut and a plastic fountain set up there, next to the pink flamingos they picked up on sale at the local hardware store.

For a few years they seemed to be making a little money. They bought a color television and a meat freezer, and a new monument for their mother's grave outside the village. There were no other relatives to spend money on, and neither of them ever went out. They didn't drink or smoke, but sometimes sat all night before the TV, sipping coffee, dragging themselves out in the morning to do the chores after a few hours of fitful, uneasy sleep.

Their habits meshed surprisingly together. Like a cog and wheel accidentally matched, they made things go with a rough motion, not altogether snug. Every morning Garnett would make breakfast. It was always fried bacon with eggs and toast, and they ate after the first milking. Walter would come in from the barn and find the table spread, Garnett listening to the country music, slumped in the new pine rocker in a kind of daze, his lips moving slightly to the words of the songs.

They ate silently, the music rambling on. Walter was slower than Garnett and sometimes he would stop and tilt his head to one side, his mouth full of breakfast. He found the songs monotonous, having acquired different tastes in the army. Something about the songs annoyed him, but he didn't know how to say so without challenging Garnett. It was like the sameness of the breakfast, which he had complained about, only to find Garnett refusing to get up for three days, just lying there in the west bedroom, staring glumly at the yellowing flower print of the wallpaper which had not been replaced in the renovations because it had been their mother's. Finally Walter had had to apologize, though sometimes he crept downstairs early, while Garnett's snores still sounded through the hall, and stuffed himself with cheese and cereal and made tea instead of coffee, because, as he told himself, it was good to have a change.

Every morning, as soon as Walter headed back to the barn, Garnett would gather up the breakfast things and begin the washing up, setting out the scraps for the dog, which he insisted be chained up every night. He would go out the side door through the old summer kitchen which was piled with trunks, to be greeted by the eager yelps of the collie as he set down the dish. Even in winter he would stand there awhile, staring out past the corner of the barn across the fields which rolled back evenly to the line of bush that marked the government lands. Then Garnett would slowly return to the kitchen and go methodically about the washing up. He was always glad to be alone, glad to have Walter out of the house. If the heat was on, he would turn it down, and turn up the music. He liked the thick-bodied voices of the country singers, especially the sad wailing of the betrayed girls, the desperate wives. He always thought of them as real people and was shocked when Walter had once shown him an article about one of the stars in a glossy magazine. It seemed ridiculous to him that people would talk about how they were making these things up and he wanted to throw the piece away, but because of the photos of the singer's legs and bare shoulders, he found it very hard. He left the magazine in the bathroom and sometimes, as he sat there, he would guiltily turn the pages, reaching out for that shining blonde hair with his fingertips and listening for Walter's footsteps downstairs as he stroked the glossy outline of a neck or thigh.

In the barn, meanwhile, Walter would feel free for a little while. He always liked to escape from the house to the steamy darkness where the warm breath of the animals licked out at him and soothed him. The barn hadn't changed much through the years and it reminded him of his childhood when he used to hide from his aunt, the one who took care of them, and was always vowing she would beat some sense and discipline into them. After his father had died, his aunt had moved away and the farm went over to Garnett, who later moved back from the factory town where had had a job as a night watchman. In the barn before he had gone to the army, Walter was taken by a sudden impulse: he had lain in the straw and beat about himself until the pleasure came in short, swift spurts, while the animals moaned and stamped down below him. If his aunt had ever caught him at that she would have killed him. Now he was free, of course, to do what he liked. Even so, when occasionally the need came on him, he listened anxiously for Garnett's fumbling hands on the door, and a kind of dizziness seized him, as if the waters dinning quietly in his ears would burst the sides of his head.

While the money lasted, they had built up their stock beyond what their father or grandfather had ever been able to afford. Ten or fifteen head of cattle flicked their tails between the stanchions or let themselves be eased and shouted out into the big field to graze, the dog streaking around them in full yelping voice. The pigs were penned in the barn wing, grubbing and snorting. Chickens fluttered in the ramshackle adjunct, or pecked across the yard like beaked bolsters. There were even a few sheep, though the horse had been sold to help pay for the new pickup, and the freezer was well-stocked with prime cuts of meat that had been slowly seasoned in the house shed, hung up and watched carefully against the rats.

So it worked out between them, the years ran in

the grooves of familiar seasons, but as usual in the country, bad times followed soon after the good. The government, they heard on the radio, had undercut farm prices, hurting above all the small farmer, and the brothers' money began to run short as the inevitable inflation built up against them.

Walter's monthly check could barely meet their needs, and they had to cut corners to pay off the interest on all the things they had bought on credit. On Sundays they would drive over to Crawford in the afternoon to Danny and Rae's fast food restaurant, or drop in there on the way back from church, but they seldom went to the city, forty miles away, where the prices were high and they always seemed to spend more than they intended. They had never gone out much anyway, but now it was unthinkable. It would have meant buying some new dress clothes and they were not ones to put up with the noise and foolishness of the dances for that matter. To see all those women bustling about and even drinking and smoking was a prospect that frightened them, though sometimes a terrible curiosity took hold, and they parked down the road from the huge concrete pile that was the Crawford recreation center, watching the cars zigzag in and out of the lot and listening to the half-choked surge of the music.

Wherever they strayed, though, they would eventually circle back to the farm, turning past Hayley's brick house at the corners, watching the lighted windows disappear behind them as they rolled deeper along the dirt track that snaked in through a maze of soaring birches. Past the big swamp, with its split-boled dying trees, past the scorched outline of the burned-out Kirkwood place, they came finally back to their own land, the house and barn and outbuildings rising out of the dark, and like the rest of the countryside, part of their familiar knowledge.

Slowly they settled in together, turning away from the world. To Walter, the past flaked off bit by bit, leaving a few bare glimpses of his unfurnished childhood. Sometimes, in the night, Garnett would hear his brother's cries surface from a dream, and would know he was back in the war zone, feeling the fire come out of nowhere to strike him down. Garnett would insist that they watch television practically all night, anything to put off being wakened by those shouts. But Walter would hate Garnett's way of slyly eyeing the full-color girls on the screen, refusing to turn the channels to the sports, and would storm out of the sitting room to the kitchen to make himself a sandwich and tea. Garnett could never stand his brother being in the kitchen, and would drag himself away from the screen and come out offering to help. But Walter would go cold, clutching the large breadknife in two hands, and slicing the meat or the cheese with a vicious downward motion, so that the table shook.

After evenings like this, the brothers would not speak for days, and one winter night, after they nearly came to blows, Walter vowed to leave. But Garnett swore he would give him not a nickel to take away, and since legally everything was his, Walter could only swallow his pride and abjectly resume his share of the never-ending routine.

Thanks to their parsimonious ways, and to the well-stocked freezer and Garnett's garden, they managed to survive the bad years without serious discomfort.

While Walter killed and cured the meat and packed the freezer with neat parcels marked with crayon, Garnett every summer planted a garden inside a well-tendered space near the barn where an old building had been torn down and the soil was rich and dark.

In the garden, surrounded by chicken wire, grew all the vegetables for their table and, in good years, a few to sell—corn and potatoes, beans and peas and asparagus, cauliflower, eggplants and onions.

Garnett watched over his garden with a tender ferocity, driving the dog and cats and chickens away, wary of the tramping cattle, spraying carefully to keep the insects off the delicate shoots. In the fall, everything that could be frozen was put away, and potatoes and other things laid down in the root cellar behind the summer kitchen.

So they survived the lean times, though they grew grayer and more silent, all the harder inside as the flesh softened around them.

But then came the final, terrible, quarrel.

It was a Sunday, in the middle of July, a day that rose up out of a black furnace of night in which the moon hardened like a steel disc. Walter felt the heat more than Garnett, barely forcing down the thick and viscous coffee, laboring across to the barn and back again after chores to collapse in breathless unease at the table. He could only pick at the bacon and eggs until Garnett, in disgust, swept the food off the table.

It was time for the Bible reading, and for this they moved over to the parlour, the room set aside for their meager formal rites, untouched since their mother's death.

The parlour, a big square room with purple drapes drawn, smelt faintly of lavender: a veneered divan covered in green and purple velvet stood against one wall, a few large chairs, and a long doily-draped table on which sat stately old pieces of china and the family Bible occupied the rest.

Stirred by the movements of their boots, dust sieved up through every coil of the decorated floor mats, only to catch fire as the heavy curtains were drawn back and daylight poured fiercely in on them. As usual, Garnett set the Bible on the low table in front of the divan and opened it to one of several dozen places marked by elaborate ribbons.

Walter sank down into one of the big chairs, sweat rising on his forehead. He was beginning to long for the cool woods, a bath in the pond, any escape from this heat. He resented Garnett's insistence that he take part in these readings, even when he didn't want to. He stared angrily at his brother's big boney hands turning the pages, at his thin body folded up like an insect's, at the long gray-fringed balding head that was shining with light, not sweat. Garnett ran his thin fingers across the oversized pages and looked up with sudden sharpness at Walter, as if he could feel his resistance. Then he began to read very slowly the sonorous cadences that he knew almost by heart.

He had chosen one of his favorite passages, the story of Joseph and Potiphar's wife. In a low, creaking voice, he read the story of Joseph's temptation, how God was with him when he went to the prison, how he interpreted the dreams of the prisoners, and later the Pharaoh's dream of the gaunt cows eating the fat cows, and of the scanty ears of corn swallowing the ripe ears of corn.

He read on and on in the stifling heat of the room and pictures rose out of the familiar sentences, pictures that shaped themselves in Walter's mind despite his resistance and discomfort. They hung there a moment, bright scenes from a childhood he had somehow forgotten, then dissolved slowly like jellied candy shapes in the heat.

Still Garnett read on, but Walter closed his eyes on the light, twisting his head away from the pictures that continued to assert themselves. He thought of the mockery of such things he had known in the army, a mockery hateful to him, but telling. The soft pulse of something strange sounded in his eardrums. It was the old trouble, he thought, the rolling of waters.

"Dead Sea waters," he found himself saying aloud. And then he laughed.

Garnett's voice sharpened to a rasp, but he continued, his fingers tightening on the book.

But Walter could stand it no longer. Slowly he got up, pushing free of the heavy cushions of the chair.

Garnett stopped reading and stared up at him.

"I've had enough," Walter said, the half-stifled words spilling out as he moved for the door.

Garnett stood up too, and he started to speak. But Walter was gone, his steps a brief thunder in the hall and kitchen.

Across the yard and straight for the barn he went, toward the cool darkness. It was time for the cows to go out to the pasture. Why should he wait in the house under the threat of his brother's anger? It was time for the cows to go out; then he could rest, and escape from the heat.

In the barn, he realized he had forgotten the dog. He would need the dog to control them. He turned back to the house. But Garnett was there, outside, staring at him, his long figure drifting vaguely toward the pickup which sat half out of the garage-shed in the boiling sunlight.

"Goddamn it then, take the truck!" Walter called at him, and spat in the dust. The dog, hearing the rare sound of a voice raised, started to bark.

Garnett turned back, a vague blue-clad figure in a

glare of sunlight, tugged at by the sharp excitement of the dog's barking.

"Goddamn it!" Walter cried out, seeing that his brother would get there first, "Take the dog, then! Read him the good book, you damned mealy-mouthed rot-preacher!"

He whirled, and headed back to the barn. By God, he would let them out anyway! He would do it without the dog.

His breath came in short gasps. The sweat ran a map of blotches over his shirt.

In the barn he plunged furiously between the stanchions, swearing again and again as he kicked at the tumbled-down bales of straw.

The cows stirred and moaned uneasily. He began to drive them one by one down the low ramp and out into the yard.

Taking fright at his speed, at his anger, at the sound of hooves crashing down on the ramp, two or three baulked, kicking and rolling in the darkness until the barn shook.

Outside, the dust plumed under the terror of the bellowing cows. The dog barked a steady staccato. Then from the bottom of a wave of darkness that seemed to take hold of him and hurl him furiously against a coil of rope, Walter heard his brother's repeated screams.

He scrambled forward toward the ramp, tripped and rolled helplessly out into the blazing sunlight. The farm jigsawed around him like a landscape of fragments.

Crawling up on his hands and knees, he saw the cows at forage in the garden, tramping and dancing and squirming between the coiled-out ruin of the fence.

His brother stood white-faced, silent now, waving his arms in a crazy semaphore of anger and despair.

Walter took some time getting the dog calmed down and working, but there was no hope at all for the garden. It had only taken them minutes to reduce it to a big, squared-off run of compost.

Garnett made no attempt to help in the roundup, but trailed back into the house, drifting past Walter, the straggling cows, and the still barking dog, without a word.

The sun fell on Walter like a pressing weight, but he laughed. He could not help it. Laughter possessed him, he shook with endless, mindless laughter as the sweat poured off him, blurring his sight and splitting his vision into a tangle of fiery threads. He rubbed at his face with gnarled, filthy hands, staring down curiously at his clothes stained with cowshit, feeling the thumps of pain from a banged-up leg. He stuck his soft belly out and laughed.

At last, with the cattle in the barn, he dragged himself into the house, into the bright kitchen where the light seemed to sing. He moved from room to room, remembering everything, the past, all the terror, the bright pictures of the Good Book, even those.

He went into the shower and washed himself clean, touching himself all over, then walking naked through the house with light, dripping steps. He sang to himself, to the music inside his head, to the tides of that music.

He dried his body at last with a big towel, dressed himself in his old army uniform, which he found at the bottom of a chest in the bedroom closet, and then went down to the kitchen and ate.

He took a thick steak from the refrigerator and grilled it carefully. He pried open a sealed jug of milk and drank until it ran over the corners of his mouth. Then he sat down and ate the steak slowly, savoring every bite. The heat in the kitchen was terrible, and the sweat ran off him in a shower. He laughed.

He went back to his room and began packing. He packed neatly a suitcase full of clothes, clothes he had not worn in twenty years, none of them work-clothes, and then went down to the kitchen and jammed in all the food he could carry, bread and cheese and big slices of cooked ham.

As he was leaving the house, an old straw hat set jauntily over his face, he saw the dog and remembered something. He put down his suitcase and tramped back into the house, whistling to himself. He walked slowly from room to room, taking everything in, but with no undue haste, lingering here and there—in the parlour, in the attic, in every upstairs room, and then finally, a little while longer in the room where his brother lay, quite motionless on the narrow bed, staring up at the ceiling.

For a brief moment the brothers looked at each other. Finally. with nothing spoken, Walter turned and made his way out of the room, down the stairs and back to where he had left his suitcase. He spat as the terrified, outraged dog leapt to the full chain's length. bellowing at the dust his heels raised across the yard.

It was Hayley's boy Jack, out walking six days later, who first heard the animals howling. Something in the steady, faint desperation of the sounds disturbed him, and he mentioned it that night to his father, who shrugged it off. Those Craig brothers were weird enough, God knows, the old man said. No telling what was going on over there, probably a prayer meeting likely as anything. They listened against the wind and rushing water and picked up a strange shrill terror of sound that made them stop and look at each other with uneasy hesitation.

"I guess we'd best go down," Hayley decided, and so they went, arriving just in time to save one or two of the starving animals. Three cows came out of it all right, although the pigs had killed each other in a vain effort to find food in that dark hot barn, and the sheep had just flopped down like big bloated sacks of wool. The dog, lucky for him, had slipped his collar and was gone.

What was up in the bedroom, though was something a little stronger. The police arrived, and a doctor, shaking his head and complaining about the stench and the folly. He was a country doctor but not used to this kind of thing, much.

They never did find out what had happened— why Garnett had wanted to drag all those packages of meat up to the bedroom to thaw out and rot while the animals were raising such a howl around him. Why he had torn up the family Bible and strewn it all over the house. How he could just lie there, gnawing at those foul parcels with all that noise going on. Or what possessed Walter to take himself out to the swamp in his army suit and sit there sweating and freezing and laughing himself crazy until they finally found him and took him away, suitcase and all.

There were no answers, of course, but in those parts, for a long time, it made quite a story.

Blue Menus

Alice leaned out of the car window to get the order. A man at the door of the burger joint whistled. Flushed with heat and acne the Kim's girl stretched down, two greasy wrapped burgers balanced on her fingertips. She turned with expert ease to sweep up the shakes and the fries.

"Check the flavours," Jay mumbled from behind the wheel. The Olds roared and rattled as his foot teased the engine up.

"One strawberry, one chocolate," said the Kim's girl, abruptly slamming the wicket. The man who had whistled stood by the entrance and watched them. A hot breath of onions and charcoal filled the car. Alice flipped down the glove compartment door and balanced the little parcels there, helping herself to the fries. A half-dozen quickly disappeared; she drew the back of her delicate hand over her perfect, greasy, pink-bow mouth.

Ferociously, Jay stubbed his cigarette. A car horn sounded behind them. In the rear-view mirror he saw a white Corvette with Clarkson inside, looking cool.

"It's Paul!" Alice turned and chirruped. "I think he's following us."

Jay stepped on the gas, swung the wheel crazily and blasted out to the road. Skidding on gravel, the Olds nudged a trash can, snaked to the inner lane.

"Don't eat all the damn fries," Jay said, adjusting his rimless glasses, on the lookout for traffic cops.

"I think Paul really likes me," Alice murmured, between sips of the milkshake.

They sped along Carling Avenue, past the motels and gas stations, then up the Queensway, suspended above a sea of neon and yellow lights. Jay sucked his shake, steering with one hand in and out of the jockeying traffic.

"I think Paul wants to make me," Alice announced, in her faint; high-pitched voice. She was already crumpling the empty shake carton and tearing at the paper-wrapped burger.

"Everybody wants to make you," he said. "I'm surprised he hasn't already."

"Maybe he has," she put it to him coyly, and tossed some paper out the window.

"Like hell he has." Jay stepped viciously on the gas pedal.

"Have some French fries," she said.

At the next exit Jay swung them raggedly into the ramp lane.

The engine roared crazily; they skidded up to a stop sign, paused for a fraction of a second, and lurched into a dark swirl of suburban parkland.

"What's happening?" Alice asked. "Aren't we going to the party?"

"Later." Jay bent forward, refusing to look at her.

After a few minutes they rattled to a stop in a large lot that was closed at one end by a tattered backstop. Jay turned off the engine and it was suddenly very dark and quiet. Empty wooden bleachers rose out of huddled shadows, planked steps rigid between the pot-holed diamond and the trees. Jay leaned over and awkwardly kissed her ears and throat.

"Don't," she said. "Let's go to the party, Jay."

He leaned further, hungrily kissing her breasts through her shirt, and when his glasses got in the way, he pulled them off and threw them on the dashboard.

"C'mon." He pulled her out of the car, reached under the seat and withdrew a small flask. "Bring the rest of the French fries," he ordered.

They settled in the grass at the foot of the bleachers, gulping down the remains of the food and passing the flask back and forth. After a while Jay unbuttoned her shirt and put both his hands on her breasts.

"Don't," she said faintly, letting him do what he wanted.

"Seventh inning stretch," he said throatily, getting her bra off and fastening his mouth on her breasts. She felt his tongue on the tips of her nipples.

"Last of the ninth," he announced, working her belt loose and sliding his left hand inside her pants.

"Don't, Jay, please don't." She lay back, feeling the whiskey take hold. She was so hungry now, she could easily have devoured two more hamburgers.

"You love me, don't you? You love me," she insisted.

But he pressed against her, glassy-eyed, moaning.

Dazed, she felt his tongue inside her mouth, his hands all over her belly and thighs. She was starving, she realized, glad this would soon be over, yet she liked it, too.

"Touch me," she said, and moved his fingers along to the right place.

2

"A nice ham," announced Lily Matson, "there's nothing nicer for a special occasion."

Her husband looked at her quizzically from the other end of the table. He held up the carving knife and it glittered, snaring the candlelight.

"Rare or well-done?" Bob Matson joked, winking at Alice.

Smiling vaguely, Alice rearranged her serviette. "The soup was very good," she declared, looking nervously across at Jay, who sniggered.

"Well, everything has to be just right for my son's engagement dinner," Lily Matson affirmed. "And, after all, it is Christmas Eve."

"It's Alice's engagement dinner too, mother," Bob Matson reminded his wife. "How wonderful to be twenty-one and as beautiful as a princess. Isn't she like a princess, Lily? Or even like one of your Playboy pinups, Terry? At least we suspect so," he added pointedly.

"Now, Bob," said Lily, looking first at her

husband, and then protectively at her younger son. "I don't think we should be talking about pinups on a family occasion like this. Besides, Alice is much better looking than any of those girls you see in the magazines.... Oh, give her lots more ham, Bob!"

"I am, sweethearr, I am. But the poor girl has to leave some room for your incredible strawberry shortcake. You wouldn't want her to cop out after the main course, would you? Now how about you, Terry, since for once you've blessed us with your presence?"

Terry stirred slightly under this needling. "It's the holidays, Dad. I've got an awful lot to do."

"It's true we don't see much of you these days, Terry," his mother chimed in.

"No wonder," Jay murmured audibly.

"Don't be rude, Jay," his father cautioned. "You're not exactly a very good example."

"I'm not the only one," Jay cut back.

Lily bustled about nervously, starting to pour the wine. "I wish the men of my family would be a little nicer to each other," she pleaded. "Why don't we all have a nice glass of this Chateau whatever it is and talk about something pleasant."

"Like the world situation," Jay couldn't resist. "Anybody heard about any good new Wars lately?"

"I was talking to Joe Byrnes about the whole question of peace," Alice put in. "He thinks it's hopeless because of our collective death wish."

"Joe Byrnes, who on earth is Joe Byrnes?" asked Lily, plumping down and staring across at her with her small birdlike eyes.

"Joe Byrnes is one of our profs," Jay explained in a bored voice. "He has long conversations with Alice about the Western World's death wish; meanwhile his wife is trying to get the kids to bed. She isn't interested in the death wish."

"That's ridiculous, Jay," said Alice sharply. "Joe takes me very seriously. He loved my essay on Nietzsche, remember?"

"When you go to a woman don't forget the whip," Terry put in.

"Is that a quote from Nietzsche?" asked his father, irritated by the shift in the conversation.

"It sure is," said Jay defiantly, adjusting his glasses. "1 ought to know. I wrote most of that essay myself."

"You damn well didn't" said Alice, really angry.

"I don't think it's right, this familiarity, calling professors by their first names and all that," said Lily, beginning to look forlorn. "Of course I never went to the university, but I do believe in respect."

"Nothing like the old virtues," said Bob, throwing his glance innocently upward.

"I did almost all the research for that paper myself," Alice insisted. "I worked out all the ideas."

"I'm sure you did, Alice," said Lily, full of sympathy.

"What use is an essay assignment about such an abstruse topic anyway?" Bob asked. "Intellectual dilettantes all over the place and the economy in such a mess. Not that I don't respect the value of learning. My degree was in English."

"I always said that was why the Prudential hired you," Lily said. "You could write a nice piece about anything.... Have some more sweet potatoes, Alice?"

"So Joe Byrnes thinks you're a cute number, Alice?" said Bob Matson with a wink and a flourish of his wine glass. "Well, you certainly are, and we're all for it, aren't we, boys?"

"This isn't the country club, Dad," Jay snapped at him. "We aren't going to sit here and leer. You remember last summer all those cronies of yours who kept gaping at—"

"Oh, come off it, Jay, don't be so puritanical," his father interrupted. "Alice is the kind of girl who attracts attention."

"What's this all about?" asked Lily, "I don't remember anything happening at the country club."

"Just Alice in a bikini," said Terry laconically.

"A thing of beauty is a joy forever," Bob went on fixedly.

Alice bowed her head. Jay brought his knife down on the table, sharply.

"Why, just look at how that ham's gone," said Lily. "We certainly didn't leave much for the next guy!"

3

"A second helping? Don't tell me you want a second helping?"

Jay, who was shoving the ice cream back in the freezer, paused.

He stared nearsightedly at his wife, who had half-risen, then flopped back down in her chair. She looked up at him with her innocent blue eyes.

"But I'm hungry, Jay, and Dr. Gold says it's fine. I've only gained twenty-nine pounds and my time's nearly up. You want me to have a healthy baby, don't you?"

"Don't be silly, Alice, that's not the point." He came around the table and tenderly patted her pink swollen arms. "I just can't wait for you to look like yourself again."

"Oh, fuck off," she said, wrenching herself up

with surprising swiftness. She took a few wobbling steps across the tiny kitchen. The chair crashed to the floor.

"I've hardly eaten anything today," she moaned at him. He blinked and stared at her incredulously.

"Oh no—only bacon and eggs and toast, a couple of Danish, morning coffee with more pastry, three chicken sandwiches, pie and ice cream, soup, steak and potatoes, more ice cream with chocolate syrup and now—"

"You don't love me," she cried, "You just don't love me."

He swept forward and took her, with some difficulty, in his arms. "I'm sorry, Alice, my God, I'm sorry. Let's not spoil the weekend with this arguing. Of course I want my baby, both my babies, to be healthy. You just go right ahead and eat all you want."

He held her, belly to belly, for a minute, then stepped back, patting his own stomach and smiling at her.

"Why I guess I'm getting just a little plump myself. Or didn't you notice?"

"As a matter of fact I did," she said coldly. "When's it due?"

He stood back sheepishly, forcing a smile. "I'm

considering an abortion."

"Can I have my ice cream now?" she asked.

4

"Coriander vichyssoise for madame," announced the waiter, setting down the little gold-rimmed plate in front of Alice.

They both waited, hypnotized, while he circled the table. "And for monsieur, the saffron mussel bisque."

The wine arrived, a Chablis bichot, and was tipped into the oversize glasses. Jay tasted and dutifully nodded his approval.

"*Bon appetite,*" said the waiter and scurried away with his assistant. Jay and Alice smiled at each other across the candlelight and the flowers.

"This vichyssoise is delicious," Alice assured him, after a few mouthfuls. "I'm so glad we took the trouble to get the baby sitter."

"Why not?" Jay waved a gracious gesture. "What's an anniversary without a celebration?"

"It's so nice to do something without Val, just by ourselves," she confided.

"He can be an awful pain in the ass."

"I didn't mean that." She looked hurt. "He's a

wonderful child."

"Of course he is...Mmm....This bisque is terrific. I must tell Louise about it. She's a great expert on French restaurants, you know."

"Which Louise is that?"

"Louise Arthur. I must have mentioned her before. She used to do the morning show with me. The one who was such a terrific tennis player. Surely I must have told you about Louise. She went on to become executive producer of the Tonight Show."

"Oh. You still see her?"

Jay wiped a few crumbs of pastry from his lips. "Now and again, not too often of course."

"Ships that pass in the night, is that it?"

"Darling, you're *annoyed*. Now don't be silly. There was never anything between Louise and me."

They sat through the usual moments of embarrassed silence as the busboy sidled up and removed the plates. The veal cordon bleu and *langoustines grillées* arrived, together with half a bottle of *Côtes de Nuits Villages*.

"It's not like Sharon Wells, now," Jay continued, working a slab of butter on the crusty fresh bread. "With Sharon you might have had something to worry about. Her poetry just sweeps me off my feet, and talk about a provocative body.... Of course I'm a happily married man—that kind of thing doesn't get through to me anymore."

Alice began to choke down her veal.

"Ah langouste, I could write a symphony about langouste," murmured Jay ecstatically, then suddenly raised his glass. "My God, I almost forgot, darling. To our fifth! Five beautiful years!"

Alice mechanically hoisted her glass. She was still drinking the white wine; despite the langouste he had switched to the red.

"I guess it could have been worse," she said.

"I didn't really forget, of course. I was just kidding."

"Do you think I look beautiful tonight?" she asked suddenly.

"Very beautiful. You've lost even more weight recently. Now just a few pounds more...."

"You mean you think I'm still too fat?" She turned the wine glass round in her hand. "I've been doing those damned exercises for a year and you think I'm still too fat?"

"Should I have ordered the *Fiole du Pape*?" Jay wondered aloud, reaching out to calm her with a pat of his hand.

"I can't believe it," she said. "I can't believe I'm married to you."

Jay perked up at once. "Listen," he said, "I

know you're not serious, but really, it could be a lot worse. You remember Jill Ericson, the one who used to play first base at the old diamond where we screwed around as kids? Well, you know she became a model and was terrifically successful. No wonder, such a beautiful lady, right? Anyway, she married this guy and he turned out to be gay. You thought it was only in the movies? She told me all about it over lunch a few times."

"You've been seeing Jill as well? Don't you ever eat lunch alone?"

"To tell you the truth—I don't want to hide anything from you—I actually took her to dinner."

Alice's fingernails sawed at the tablecloth. "While I'm sitting at home, minding Val and cleaning the house, you've been zipping around town with these ladies. I can't believe you, Jay! You're a thousand times worse than your father. I actually have some sympathy for poor stupid Lily. I'm going to leave you, Jay, I hope you realize that."

Voices dipped at a nearby table; the maitre d' looked up from his post at the far end of the velveted room.

"For God's sake let's not go into it here," Jay begged her. He reached out quickly and patted her arm. "Listen, for dessert I'm going to have the herb cheesecake; and I want you to taste the *ananas au rhum*—I know you'll love them. Why don't we order the champagne now as well.... You remember, when we were kids we promised ourselves champagne at least once a week after we were married. We have some catching up to do."

"I don't want any goddamned champagne."

"Hey, c'mon, you can't drink water. This is our anniversary! Maybe you'd rather have a red? You know, last week Maureen Chantal introduced me to a great Bordeaux she discovered in a French restaurant in France! I'm sure you remember Maureen: she was the ballerina who was working on her Ph.D....I used to....Hey, where are you going? Alice!"

Alice stirred, turned round in her chair, but she didn't get up. She looked helplessly at Jay, at the candle-points gleaming in his eyeglasses: two blips of light on her own reflected, doubled face.

5

"You're so beautiful tonight, I love you," Jay murmured, hovering close to her, kissing her ear.

Contentedly smiling, she sank back into the pillows.

"You're perfect, adorable. You know how much

I've always loved that blue dress. Your body is magnificent—the dress shows it perfectly. No one would suspect you're nearly forty. You look barely twenty-five. My God, I could see how crazy all the men were for you. They could hardly keep their hands off you tonight."

She laughed a happy little silver laugh. "But the reception was for you, Jay. You're the one who's getting the big promotion. They were all just being polite to the wife of the new superstar."

He jumped up, genuinely taken aback. "Why, that's ridiculous, darling, and you know it. I owe everything to you. You've been my muse, my inspiration."

He collapsed on the couch, kissing her breasts and her neck, his hands reaching up for her thighs. She wriggled elusively, kissed him.

His lips found her mouth in a passionate kiss. They clawed and writhed awkwardly, as if drowning together. When they surfaced she looked at him fondly with glittering eyes.

"Shouldn't we have something to eat, Jay? I think maybe we're both just a little high and a little drunk."

"Of course, darling, and you know, I promised to make dinner tonight—this very special night. It's just that I can hardly tear myself away from you. I want you so badly; I've never wanted you more."

"You're so sweet. Why don't I just throw together a little snack. It'll only take a few minutes."

He sat back stiffly. "Oh no, I wouldn't hear of it. This is something I've wanted to do for you for a long time. But there is one little thing, darling—I nearly forgot. I hope you don't mind. I did invite some people over to join us. I'm so angry about that now. I want so much to have you all to myself."

She sat up, slightly crestfallen. "Oh, you didn't! Isn't there any way we can get out of it? Surely we don't need anybody tonight of all nights. Isn't there anything we can do about it, Jay?"

He crossed the room slowly to the antique side table where they had left their half-empty glasses of champagne. He filled up the glasses carefully and carried them back to the couch.

"I really think it would be awkward to cancel out now, darling. But never mind. I should get to work on the meal."

"Who's coming, anyway, Jay? Who on earth did you invite?"

He took a discreet sip of the champagne. "Listen, I want everything to be a surprise. I don't want you to worry your pretty head about these things. Just leave it all to me."

He leaned across and kissed her passionately on the mouth.

She stood up and they exchanged another long kiss. He took her glass very gently out of her hand and set it down on the coffee table with his own. His breath came in short little gasps. He began to unfasten her dress.

"Oh Jay, please don't. There isn't time now."

"Nonsense."

She stood there, quite glassy-eyed, swaying from side to side as he fumbled at her dress. It fell to the floor and she stepped out of it carefully. She was wearing high heels and a black bra and panties.

"My God, you're beautiful."

He kissed the cleft of her breasts, then her shoulders. He fell to his knees, rubbing his cheek on her thighs; he ran his tongue over the little fuzz of blonde hair on her stomach.

She kicked off her shoes. Clumsily, he pulled off her bra and panties while she wriggled about, half-resisting. She stood there, her body soft pink in the lamplight.

"I want you," he murmured in a strangled voice.

She was suddenly, blushingly shy. "But Jay, I've got to call the camp and see how Val's doing. And your guests must be coming soon. It's insane....

You've got to cook dinner. Oh my God!"

He was touching her, kissing her, his mouth all over her body. She buckled and bent, her arms wrapped around him.

"I want you," he muttered in a voice raw and broken.

She swooned back. Roughly, he grabbed at her, sweeping her up in his arms. He half-carried her, half-dragged her across the room into the dimly lit, carpeted hall. She saw how his eyes shone with excitement and felt the wild beat of his pulse as he touched her.

"Where are we going, Jay? What are we doing? This is mad."

They staggered and groped their way into the kitchen. A long low breakfast table ran nearly the length of the room. In a quick glance, before he pushed her down on the table, she saw the dishes and candles, the serviettes and the cutlery piled on the counter.

"Jay!"

He sat her there, kissing and licking her, his hands all over her body. Her head tilted back helplessly, she stared at the bare white ceiling.

"I want you," he gasped. "I want you more than anything in the world."

She closed her eyes dreamily; he was suddenly gone from her.

Gently, she swayed up, balancing herself on the edge of the table with weak outstretched hands.

When she looked at him, drowsily, she saw that he had taken off his jacket and now hovered there, cradling a familiar oversized bottle of olive oil. His eyes shone and his tongue moved across his dry lips.

She suddenly snapped from her dream.

"Jay, look at me! What are you doing? You're crazy!"

His eyes were glazed over with a new kind of hardness.

Methodically, he rolled up his sleeves, then forced her back down on the table.

"You're my meat now," he said with harsh tenderness.

She felt herself held there. Oil streamed over her skin, cold then warmer as he slapped at her thighs and her stomach.

She opened her mouth to protest, but his hands worked all the faster, caressing her shoulders and breasts, making hard firm strokes across her body. It was like being laid out and opened up to have a baby, she thought, only no pain, just the helplessness of being stretched naked on a table. No pain at all, only pleasure.

When the pleasure came stronger, it made her sleepy. It was as if his fingertips secreted the oil, which ran on her skin and subdued her.

"Jay..." It was all she could do to get out his name, to force open her eyelids. His glance lay on her like a weight; she closed her eyes.

"My sweet lamb," she heard him coo, "my baby, my precious."

A vague tender feeling possessed her. It was nothing like having a baby, no, she was the baby: she was slipping away back to childhood, and she wanted to cry out, to gurgle. She felt the soft moans rising in her throat, felt her body dissolve as he touched her.

She longed to touch him, to hold him, then he seemed to be gone, but he touched her. He touched her thighs and buttocks, reached up between her spread legs. His tongue probed, then his teeth. He was biting her shoulders and breasts, forcing her to a climax.

The pleasure consumed her; she lay there writhing, her mind swallowed up in a wild flood and frenzy. Slowly, as her intimate screams died, she became aware that he was no longer touching her, that he had suddenly left her, that the kitchen was empty.

She started to speak, against the insistent ringing of chimes, and opened her eyes wide. Her body felt full and prepared. The white ceiling above her had started to move, to revolve with immense and meaningful slowness.

Then she heard Jay's voice in the hall, raised in greeting, and the silvery eager laughter of women.

The Well

Tamara Ellison's thirteenth-floor apartment in the Severn Building was nothing special, but it did have a downtown location and a fine view of Ottawa's Museum of Science. That old building, with its high limestone facades and appealing Gothic windows, was somehow reassuring. On some mornings, as she stood at the window of her kitchen drinking coffee, it seemed to anchor her.

As a young student she'd started out in a single room in an old house full of university women in an even nicer part of town, but when she fell in love the place quickly became claustrophobic. Too many bodies, too many parties, women shrieking with laughter, young men thumping around, and the kitchen always filthy and disorganized. She'd been almost embarrassed to take her French professor there, for although they were lovers and had even gone to Paris together, the clutter and the lack of privacy began to wear on them both.

One day she came home to her room to find her friend Sally in bed with a graduate student. Tamara's dresses, which Sally had obviously been trying on for the young man, were scattered about, and a half-empty bottle of wine sat on the bedside table. Tamara moved out the next week and took a one-room apartment in the Severn, where she suddenly felt free and independent.

For a while it was glorious to have Yves all to herself in her little flat, which, as an art student, she decorated with imagination and skill. She often gave him drinks and dinner; then they took the phone off the hook and went to bed. Mornings they would head off to classes, usually separately. Their relationship was intense and promised to go on forever; she felt almost married. Some months later, however, he began to appear less frequently, and when he did, he often seemed distant and abstracted. Then one day he informed her (by telephone) that it was over between them. Tamara found out from Sally that he had taken up with a blonde French professor who had studied with Foucault and had worked as a topless dancer while she finished her Ph.D., which was based on some new feminist theory concerning the uselessness of male mentors.

Tamara fell into a depression. It went on for months; she saw no one and did only the minimum on her courses. Her mother said she would come out of it, and when she didn't, Mrs. Ellison recommended her own therapist, a Doctor Asgard, who, after a few innocuous consultations, got Tamara to take a special drug, and began to have sex with her during their sessions at his apartment-office.

At first distracted and vaguely stirred, Tamara soon fell into a deeper sadness. Somehow she managed to finish her degree, and went on to do graduate work. Yet Asgard continued to hold her in his spell; she simply couldn't break with him, and her mother—who knew nothing of their sexual connection—assured her that he would help her in the long run. Two years later Tamara got a job in the Heritage Department, and managed to dump her therapist, or as she privately named him, the rapist. She kept in touch with Sally, made a few casual female friends, but never moved out of the Severn. Her only companion was Midnight, her black cat, an animal she had rescued from the pound. One day she woke up, aged forty-five, and found herself fighting breast cancer. Many painful months later she was declared free from it, but on the day the doctor told her the good news, Midnight disappeared. She was heart-broken, but remained in the apartment. It was only on her sixtieth birthday, after some renewed contact with Sally, that she finally found the courage to make a change.

It happened that her job involved doing research on historic buildings, and one morning she came upon a file with a property for rent in the hills just north of the city—an old post-and-beam house with a big lot, a splendid porch, and nice views. The next day she drove up to take a look.

She wasn't disappointed. The place was barely twenty minutes from the city, up a low sloping hill on a dirt road, with only a small log cabin for company. The cabin had been built at the next turn of the road, and was only just visible from the house. The road was enclosed by deep woods; in the early spring the maples and birch were not yet thick-leafed, but clumps of evergreens made for a soft arboreal darkness. Tamara could see trails winding among the pines, into that darkness, and thought how wonderful it would be to walk in a wood that began just a few feet from her front door.

The house itself looked inviting, with gray stone walls, a fine long porch, and a roof of green tiles. The well, which she found not far from an old maple tree, on the left side of the house, was apparently being worked on. The cover had been pulled off and a large green pump mechanism and handle lay beside it in the grass. She walked over to the edge of the shaft and peered down. A gleam of light revealed the water below, deeper than she expected. Tamara shivered and backed away. She made a note to find out why the cover had been removed and what was being done—after all, the water taps in the house had worked perfectly well. Perhaps the roots of the tree had begun to pull the bottommost stones of the well apart.

After her first inspection, she had started to walk toward the road when a battered old pickup truck came roaring and grinding up the hill. As the vehicle passed her, a grim-faced man wearing a black Stetson peered out from the cab. His long, pale face and dark moustache caught her attention; she thought he looked vaguely familiar. She watched as he pulled up at the nearby cabin, to be greeted by a big dog and a small woman in a red shirt and jeans who came out and stood waiting, but whose face she couldn't see.

She ought to go over and introduce herself, she thought, but something made her hesitate. After all, she hadn't really decided to take the place, had she?

She shrugged her shoulders and walked up one of the nearby trails. The next hour she spent exploring the surrounding woods and fields. She returned to take a final look at the house. She was delighted with everything.

After that, she got in her car and started home. Driving back, she was very excited. Of course she would rent the house! The place was quite reasonable, and she could afford to keep her apartment in town as well, for a while at least. This retreat would make a perfect summer place, and she didn't have to commit herself to a long rental, at least not until the fall. Everything seemed encouraging; quite perfect, really. She was making a change in her life at last— but she must remember to check on that well.

The next day she looked over the files on the house again, and inquired around, but no one knew anything about any repairs or water problems. But what did it matter, really? The office records showed the place to have an unspectacular and solid history. Built by an Irish farming family, it had been occupied for years by a series of respectable civil servants. Tamara made arrangements to rent it, contacted a local trucker, and a week later had most of her things moved up there. A perfect place to settle, and to have a home office. Her first days in the country were blissful.

She had never lived outside of the city or suburbia, and found everything transforming. By day she could walk up the trails, enjoying the play of sunshine on the leaves, or drive down to eat lunch by the river. At night, a lovely silence descended, boundless and healing. She sat on her porch in the moonlight, or wandered out to look at the stars. She woke to see squirrels and rabbits run in the yard; she heard the songs of birds. She realized that for nearly her whole life she had been living in a kind of claustrophobia, pressed upon by machinery and people, by her own sad thoughts, her limitations. This was different; it was like being released or reborn.

When she looked at herself in the mirror each morning she saw, despite the wrinkles, the gray hairs, the extra weight, a woman with shining eyes and a kind of dark beauty; a woman whose body, despite its past suffering, seemed to be blooming again. Soon she walked with a quicker step; her eyes were full of light and hope. People in the office began commenting on her transformation.

The summer came on; everything around seemed to flourish, to grow richer and deeper. All her routines were more pleasant, more rewarding. Then one night, as she was sitting in her kitchen after dinner listening to some gentle music on her Mp3 player, she heard a noise on the porch, a tiny crash as if one of her plants had been toppled. *That dog,* she thought, *that dog from the cabin.* The big half-collie up the road occasionally wandered down and prowled around her yard, perhaps looking for rabbits.

She had never introduced herself to the couple up there, never exchanged a word with them. Occasionally they passed her on the road, always driving too fast, always staring at her, but they never once stopped or waved a greeting. It was unnatural, she thought, but she just couldn't bring herself to make the first move. Besides, everything had been so perfect here, so peaceful and free of obligations, she just didn't want to deal with them.

She got up and went to the front door. She listened, and heard a sound that surprised her, one that made her stop and hold her breath. It was the distinctive, rather pitiful meowing of a cat.

Tamara flung the door open, and there, on the lighted porch, she saw a large black cat, stretching its legs and gazing up at her, its glittering green eyes fixed on hers.

"*Midnight!*" she whispered to herself, then stepped back and pressed her hand to her mouth, peering around the shadowy porch, as if someone might have overheard her foolishness.

The cat cried out mournfully, seemingly demanding to be let in. Tamara stepped aside and watched it parade past.

She closed the door quickly and stood there for a moment in a daze.

Of course it wasn't Midnight; it couldn't be. Midnight was dead. But cats, she knew very well, aroused strange thoughts, and carried strange associations. Almost as if by instinct, as if under orders from elsewhere, she went to the refrigerator and poured out a bowl of milk for the animal.

The next few weeks were very odd. The cat took up residence, establishing all the rituals between them that she knew so well. Tamara accepted this, but with a kind of embarrassment, not confiding in Sally or in anyone at work. It was as if she had permitted a disreputable lover to live with her and did not want anyone to know. She hesitated to invite anyone to her house, telling herself that she could not bear to discuss the cat with them. At the same time, her relations with the animal were slightly odd; she hesitated to address it as "Midnight," yet no other name seemed appropriate.

Then one day everything took a new turn. The cat

disappeared. For three days she looked out for it, but the animal was nowhere to be found. She was both relieved and anxious. But things got worse. On one of her late afternoon walks she stopped at a favourite spot, a large boulder at the edge of a field where wildflowers bloomed, a sheltered, pretty place from which she could catch a glimpse of the river winding through the valley far below.

As she looked for a foothold to help her climb the boulder, she saw something lying in the grassy path at her feet. She gasped and shrank back, then slowly approached it, and bent over for a closer look. All at once she felt sickened, seeing what appeared to be the remains of an animal, a squirrel, a rabbit, or perhaps even a cat, recently attacked and torn to shreds, guts and skin smeared across a tangle of scrub bush.

She moaned, looked around helplessly, then hurried back to the house, fearful and at the same time angry, her mouth full of the taste of disgust.

What if those remains, that horrible torn flesh, had been her cat? And, indeed, something told her, some inner conviction, that it was her cat, that it must be her cat. The poor creature, she thought, the poor mauled beast! How could such a thing happen? Back in her kitchen she burst into tears, feeling helpless, impotent, and abandoned.

After a while, however, she began to recover, forcing herself to make some tea. As she sat down to try to drink it, she came to a conclusion. The idea flashed on her with complete suddenness and certainty. It was that dog that had done it, her neighbours' giant bastard collie! The dog, she knew, hated the cat, and had chased the poor thing a few times up the maple tree beside the well. It was a vicious animal, unfriendly always, and even threatening. The time had come, surely, to see that pair up the road and complain about it. They were just as bad as their dog, unfriendly and nasty, she was certain of it. Now she was determined to face them out.

Tamara pushed the tea aside, poured herself a small glass of Scotch from a bottle she'd stowed away, and swallowed it rather quickly. Then she fetched her favourite light green cashmere sweater and buttoned it on over her thin blouse. She didn't want that man's eyes on her body while she was taking him to task.

Walking up the road she kept waiting for the dog to run out, to start his uproar. He usually hung around the dingy shed beside the cabin. She got all the way to the front door, however, without encountering him. Though the battered old truck was in the driveway she wondered if anyone was at home. Everything looked so quiet, almost desolate, in the sunshine.

The cabin door was massive; there was no bell, only an ancient rusted door knocker. She hammered, timidly at first, then more insistently. Something stirred inside, then the door opened.

The man materialized from the shadows inside. He wore jeans and a heavy wool shirt of red plaid that wrapped him like a skin. The sleeves of his shirt were torn and caked with mud. A damp, sour smell issued from his clothes and from the cabin. There was no sign of the dog, or the woman.

"What d' you want?" he asked, his flat voice barely audible. Firelight flickered behind him in the big room. His dark eyes kept watching her.

Tamara took a deep breath, and forced herself to stand still. His rough, pockmarked skin, his untidy moustache that half-hid his thin lips, and the two ugly scars on his right cheek disturbed her. His eyes were cold and expressionless. Once again, he seemed oddly familiar, like a figure from a half-forgotten dream.

"My cat...I'm looking for my cat."

The man continued to watch her, but said

nothing. She wondered if he'd even understood.

"I live down there," she said, pointing to her house, which just then looked somehow forlorn. "My cat's wandered away somewhere. I wondered if your dog might have—"

"No, not here," he told her in the same dull monotone. "Something must have taken her. My collie's gone too. Something in the woods maybe. My wife's gone down to the city to get another. Can't live here without a dog." He hesitated, then started to turn away. "I have to be cooking my dinner now."

"Oh, yes," she mumbled. He was shutting the door on her. She felt very foolish, but also relieved to be escaping. "Goodbye, then," she added quickly, and retreated. She heard the door clamp shut behind her.

She hurried away down the road, glancing back a few times at the cabin. If his wife was in town, why was their wretched truck still in the driveway? A few wild thoughts possessed her, but she had almost reached her own doorstep when she remembered where she had seen his face.

No, she decided, *it couldn't be.*

She stood in a daze by the well and the big maple tree. Her glance rested for a moment on the old well cover, and she saw that a shovel, a full-sized garden spade with a bright red handle, had been left lying in the grass nearby. She hadn't noticed it before. Had someone been digging there?

Alarmed, she broke into a run, crossed the porch and stumbled into her house. She fumbled around in the kitchen until she found the whiskey, poured herself a large glass, and swallowed it down.

It was insane; she must be imagining things.

Desperately, she was trying to remember where she had stored her old files and clippings. Had she brought them here, or left them all at work? She climbed the stairs, flipped the light on in her office, and began to search. But after rummaging through a few boxes and examining the bulky folders in her filing cabinet, she gave up. Of course she must have left them at work.

She sat down, her breath coming fast, her thoughts wild and unfocused. Then she had an idea. Sally! Sally would remember; she was sure of it.

As she groped for her cellphone, Tamara began to feel guilty. She hadn't invited Sally up here yet, though she'd made vague promises to do so. It was awkward. Though they weren't that close any more, she knew Sally had felt neglected and a little disappointed in her. Nonetheless, she had to talk to her now. Tamara's hands trembled as she pressed the buttons on the phone.

Sally answered right away in her usual forthright voice, and Tamara greeted her, trying not to sound anxious. Clinking glasses, laughter, and some clatter could be heard in the background; she started to apologize for the interruption, but Sally brushed this off. It was all right, she said. She explained that she was in a restaurant. "I thought you might want to talk to me," she added.

Puzzled, Tamara decided not to pursue this. "Listen, Sally, I have to ask you...brace yourself, this is a rather odd question. You remember our old classmate Lorraine Judson? The pretty little one who was a court journalist and who was murdered up here in the hills all those years ago? She became the lover of that horrible convict guy.... You remember?"

"Of course I remember, Tamara. How could I forget? What about her?"

"It's not her. It's him. Did you ever hear that he got out of prison?"

There was a long pause at the other end. Tamara waited.

"No, I don't think so. I don't remember hearing anything more about him. Except that he was beaten up badly by his cellmates. They mauled him good, that bastard! Thank God for that at least."

Tamara swallowed and said nothing. She remembered that she hadn't locked her door downstairs.

Sally spoke again. "Are you okay? You know when you called I thought it was about Yves. I thought you might want to talk about it."

Tamara's thoughts wrenched away, into a new, strange channel.

"What do you mean? What about Yves?"

There was another long pause on the other end. "Oh, God, what an idiot I am! You haven't heard, have you? Poor baby, I'm sorry to have to tell you this. Yves drowned a few weeks ago at some beach over in France. That wretched blonde witch called me yesterday; she's been trying to get hold of you. It seems there's a service planned at the University.."

Tamara held the phone at arm's length and looked at it. The news came strangely through this disembodied, curious instrument. *Yves dead.* Yves, whose love had first imprisoned her, then put her in mourning for her lost life.

Sally's voice squeaked incomprehensibly, mouse-like, from the innocent, arm's-length metal.

"It's all right," Tamara said, holding the phone

close again. "It isn't your fault. And I'm not that upset. But I have to go now. I'll call you tomorrow. Don't worry about me. I'll call you."

She snapped off the phone without waiting for an answer.

She lay down on the rug, closed her eyes, and listened for a while to her own beating heart.

Yves was gone. So many times, through the years, her thoughts had returned to him, with sadness, in anger, and in resignation. She had never stopped believing that if their time together had only been different, everything would have changed for her. Now it was over; it was too late.

After a while she struggled downstairs, locked the front door, poured herself another glass of whiskey, carried it back to her bedroom, swigged it down, then suddenly burst out weeping. Long minutes passed; she controlled herself, and managed to crawl, fully dressed, into bed. After some tossing and turning, assaulted by memories, she fell into a long, fitful sleep.

She was awakened by a familiar sound, a shrill cry, relentless, insistent. It seemed to come from outside the house, from the porch perhaps. A cat, unmistakably. Had Midnight, or his double, returned from oblivion?

Tamara dragged herself up, feeling the whiskey in her head and in her stomach. It was dark. She groped her way into the kitchen, the cat's cry all the louder, much closer now. No, she hadn't been dreaming.

She peered out the window, but nothing stirred in the glaring moonlight. The dark silver landscape seemed frozen. Cupping her hands, she gathered water from the tap, splashed some on her face, then moved cautiously to the front door. She listened for a moment, then slowly turned the key and opened it.

The night was a little chilly, the porch quite empty. She paused, and once again heard the cat's plaintive cry. Where was it hiding?

Shivering a little, she crossed the porch with dreamlike steps and turned into the yard. There in the moonlight, she saw the well, the red shovel lying nearby, the clumped gloom of the bushes, and the dark, lustrous grass flowing out from beneath the shadowy trees. There was no sign of the cat.

"Midnight?" she called out, hopefully, and waited. The cry came again, apparently from the well itself.

She paused, took a step forward, stopped, then giggled, thinking, *Pussy's in the well.* She shook with half-suppressed, nervous laughter, fighting off spasms of fear.

At the round lip of the well, she stopped. The cat cried again and its plaintive voice seemed to rise from the stone walls of the shaft.

Tamara bent forward, got down on her knees, then lay flat on her stomach. She peered into the well, rubbing her eyes, trying to see through the darkness, the speckled shadows, to the very bottom.

As she stretched out her arms to grab hold of the rough stone, an image took shape in the wavering light far below her. It was not her cat that she saw, however, not Midnight's dark shape, but a melting, shifting human face. She blinked as the image transformed and brightened. *It couldn't be.* It was an illusion, surely—the light of the moon in the water.

She bit her lip and, determined now, peered into the depths of the well. *Yes, she could make it out.* It was a face, a young man's face, once familiar. She jumped to her feet, covered her eyes with her hands and stood there sobbing. Seconds later, abruptly, she stopped. Leaves rustled behind her and she turned.

A figure walked toward her in the moonlight. It was the tall man in the soiled red shirt. He had picked up the shovel and was shifting it slowly from hand to hand as he approached. She started to cry out, to speak, but choked on her words. He said nothing, but when he came closer she read in his lost look, in his bleak empty eyes, her own lifelong hopelessness and pain.

The Acrobats

My grandmother told me this story before she died. She spoke in a rather quiet voice, sitting up stiff-backed in her bed in the nursing home, her white hair pulled neatly into a bun, her wrinkled hands waving about for emphasis.

Every once in a while, perhaps at what seemed to her the important parts, a kind of flickering light came suddenly into her mild old eyes.

She was nearly ninety then, but claimed she had never mentioned these events to anyone else, though, as she confessed, the scenes had burned in her mind since childhood—a childhood spent, one might say, in another world. I report it here in her own words, with only a brief postscript for epitaph.

"You're the one who has to hear this," she began, leaning forward a little and clearing her throat, as I fetched her a glass of water from the bedside table. "You're the most sensible girl in the family, Kate. I'm awfully glad you're doing science now. My career in science went quite well, as you know. Now just pull up that chair and don't interrupt me. I don't like to be interrupted."

"Your mother may have gabbled a bit about my girlhood times, though probably all the important things were left out. She was never very interested in those old days, nor in me either if it comes to that.

"I grew up, as you know, in Williamsburg, Ontario, not much of a town really, for all the later ballyhoo about the St. Lawrence Seaway and the blessed farmers and all that rot. We've driven down there more than once—you remember I pointed out the house? A beautiful place even now, I think, though they've done everything they can to ruin it.

"In those days of course there was no siding, and the gingerbread hadn't been out off to save painting it; and the veranda ran right around the house, with none of it shorn so's they could stuff firewood in the cellar. A fine high brick mansion it was, with four or five guest rooms nearly always full—for you know my father, who was the town blacksmith, kept the house as an inn, and travellers between Montreal and Kingston used to spend the night there because the food was good, the rooms very comfortable, and the company pleasing.

"One of my earliest memories is the big fire blazing away in the front parlour. Hannah and Mary, the village girls who worked with Mother, always kept it roaring bright, even in and summer, and I used to sit there telling stories about crusaders knights to my rag dolls, while Mother directed everything from the kitchen and some well-mannered plump traveller, on his way to buy lumber or sell sewing machines, tossed me a shiny new coin from far away with the picture of the old queen stamped on it.

"Father, of course, did the outside work. He tended the horses, cleaned the stables, cut wood, kept everything in repair, and bought or traded for supplies from the farmers. He was a big man, as swarthy and dark as my mother was fair, and in the house he always seemed awkward, or even shy. Mother ruled everything from the kitchen, keeping us children on the move, for as soon as we were old enough we all helped run the place.

"There were five of us. Robert, the oldest, worshipped my father, and like him, soon retreated outside. The three girls—my two older sisters, Jane and Emma, and myself—settled down as the princesses by the fireside, though we worked very hard for the privilege. One of the things we did, for many years, was to take care of our little brother, Thomas, mother's favourite.

"He was a bright thing, with curly blond hair, shiny blue eyes and the strangest dreamy manner you can imagine. When you first looked at him, especially if he was sitting in the parlour on his rocking horse, or in the swing out back underneath the cottonwoods, you'd have felt sure that at some point he'd just spring up and go dancing away, he moved so lightly. Thomas never danced, though, and he seldom really smiled. He had been born badly-formed, with a tiny humped back and thin limbs the doctor said would never grow into a proper manly shape.

"Thomas didn't think like the rest of us, either. He was slow-minded and dreamy, though by no means stupid or incapable of learning. We all treated him in different ways! Mother protected him and coddled him; father was careful and correct—I think now he was afraid his own emotions would get out of hand— and Robert just loved the boy dearly, as did Emma and Jane.

"As for me, I fought with him and was jealous of him (after all, he had robbed me of my privileged position as the youngest). I tried to teach him things, and often got angry when I found out he knew much that I couldn't possibly know—things that had to do with the feelings of the horses, the moods of the weather, how to stitch leather so it would hold, or to read the Bible so that you understood the hidden meanings behind the quaint words. All the while he would tease me in his funny way and sometimes I got so furious that I wanted to hit him, though of course I never did.

"Except for Thomas, all of us children went through the usual experiences of those days. We worked hard at home, but were sent pretty regularly to the little one-room schoolhouse at the west end of town. On Sundays we trooped along to the Anglican church, sang, and silently asked God's mercy in curing our afflicted little brother. Though he soon dropped out of school, Thomas always came to church with us and got so interested in the sermons that he began reading our big family Bible on his own.

"Amazed by this, almost taken aback, father at last bought him a fancy bound copy of the scriptures, ordering it specially from Montreal and presenting it to the boy on his tenth birthday.

"I'll never forget the look in his eyes when he got that Book: it almost seemed that he had spent all that hard labour of years learning to read just so as to look into those pages. After chores (of which he did his carefully allotted share) he carried that leather and gilt volume away to his favourite window seat (the one that had a view of the apple orchard on the little rise west of the house), and there would recite all his treasured stories, his lips moving quickly, as if he were having a conversation with some invisible presence, hovering just outside the shining, flawed window panes.

"Really, it seemed, the book helped him. He had been born with a happy, carefree temperament. When he was very small, I remember, he would laugh often. The first time Muriel, our house cat, jumped into his crib to take a look at him, he howled with laughter, as if he had been visited by some outlandish, strange being. My mother told me that late at night when she was rocking him by the fireside he would often smile and murmur things to himself or to the guests; he was very alert then, and the travellers sitting with a last glass of port would talk to him, and ask aloud what could be going on in his tiny head. They must have been amazed at the contrast between the twisted body and the quick eager spirit.

"When he grew older, though, the village children, my playmates, did not respond to him with any such sentiments. They teased him unmercifully, until Robert threatened even the biggest of them with dire punishment if they wouldn't leave him alone. Pretty soon, with all of us on his side, and because Father was a man so much respected, and even feared, because of his strength and his silence, they relented. But there must have been very bad days for him, for notes were passed and comical drawings appeared, and once Mrs. Paterson, the wife of the United Church minister, even had the cheek to ask my mother when we would be sending him away for safe keeping to a home or a hospital.

"By the time he was seven or eight Thomas was a strange, sad child, quite cut off from everyone outside of the family, and increasingly remote, even from us. That's why the reading and the gift of the Bible seemed so perfect; at last he had a world to enter into and explore, a world full of bright, clear landscapes, where in villages with wonderful names, inhabited by vivid, passionate people, the common objects that we all loved—bread and salt, wheat and honey, fine woven cloth and the large stone jars in the kitchen—became magical, and even holy. We all understood that, I guess, though it was only later that I could think to express it, so we were happy to see him lost in that world, beginning to smile again, and to talk to us about the things he was discovering in those moments by the orchard window.

"So it went until the day of Robert's happiest birthday. (At that time Thomas was not yet twelve; and I was just a year older). Robert was all of seventeen, and for a long time he had had his heart set on owning a horse, and, sure enough, on the great day my father appeared, leading a beautiful palomino mare, already fitted out with a fine western saddle he had picked up from the Wallaces over by Chesterville.

"It was a beautiful day in early spring, and I remember how, in the little wagon yard, we crowded excitedly round while the horse stamped and snorted, rather nervous at all the fuss. Then a couple of guests came out and smoked their cigars and watched us, congratulating Robert and affirming that they hadn't seen a finer piece of horse flesh between Montreal and Belleville.

"Of course we all wanted to ride her, especially us girls, I think, for there's something very exciting about swinging up on the back of a strange, gentle animal that's nonetheless jibbing a little and blowing steam in the chilly air of a fine spring day. I guess we imagined ourselves cantering once around the town, sticking out our tongues at the boys in the south end, then dismounting, to show off a white flare of skirt, while the whole world looked on and we landed gracefully in father's strong arms. How delighted we would have been at everyone's amazement in the face of our sheer bravado!

"But in those days, fancy was one thing and the rules were another. Father just told us to behave ourselves and began to give lucky Robert a few pointers, until our brother, so unfairly skilled and well-advanced already in the art of playing cowboy, went galloping off down the road toward Bouck's Hill, just to show those Ditmars girls that he had more to offer than his strong arms, broad shoulders, and agreeable nature.

"The horse, who was named Lion Lady, became a favourite, and eventually even us girls did get to ride her. It was only Thomas who had to sit by and watch, and, strangely enough, I noticed that for the first time ever he began hanging around the stables, sometimes getting Robert to let him feed the mare. It was quite clear that he didn't want to be left out of our joy, that nothing in the world could have given him more pleasure than to be set up on the back of the horse, to be allowed to go trotting off into some dreamland he would make up out of our plain country roads and homely orchards.

"It wasn't to be, though; it just wasn't to be. Of course, as I see it now, there was no reason why he couldn't have ridden Lion Lady, for despite her ambitious name she was as gentle as a lamb, and anyway Thomas was very agile, despite his affliction, and would probably have ridden rings round the rest of us, all of us except Robert.

"But my father's fear, you see, prevented this from ever happening, for he was so secretly protective of his frail youngest son that he absolutely forbade any such tricks, and even warned Robert that if he allowed Thomas a ride in secret at any time, and Father found out, the horse would be taken from him for a summer at least, possibly forever.

"The upshot was, I would often see Thomas mooning about the stables, sitting up in the loft and just watching, feeding the mare and quietly talking to her, leaning against her and all but swinging up on her back, but nonetheless never disobeying our father's injunction, which had the force of law in the far-off days in which these things happened.

"By the end of the summer it was clear to me

that Thomas was quite obsessed with our father's prohibition, quite downcast by the whole business and that he was trying hard not to make an evil thing of something that was capable of giving him such great joy.

"To my shame—when I think of it even now I feel badly—I didn't help him at all, but was piqued by his moods and even taunted him, telling him not to be such a little sad-face, that if he studied his lessons, read his Bible and went to church with a heart unburdened by envy, he would surely rise above the temptation that had him in its grip.

"Then one day, just at the end of that summer, we had a great surprise in those parts. There was a little circus troupe travelling from town to town along the river. They gave a performance in Morrisburg, a few miles away, and to our great joy all us children were allowed to go.

"It was lovely; they had wagons and horses, a small but beautiful candy-striped tent; strange poles and wires that they set up at precarious angles, and a lean black panther they claimed had come all the way from Africa.

"There was also a clown like a Harlequin, with a beaming painted face and a yellow suit all sewn over with red diamond cloth. He did tricks and tumbles, jumped wildly at every drumbeat, and fell deftly into puddles, or to our amazement entangled himself in coils of rope that moved on the sawdust like snakes. There was a beautiful blonde lady who wore shockingly little and swung on the bars with a handsome mustached man, whose white teeth flashed in a leer every time he stepped forward for a bow. There was a magician who plucked the most amazing things from a seemingly empty grain sack—rabbits and bouquets and silk handkerchiefs and even a big purple umbrella. There was a master of ceremonies, and candy floss, jellied apples, maple sticks, ice cream and roast corn.

"We children were just in heaven. Even so, the best was yet to come. It seemed that the Valley season was over for the troupe—Morrisburg being the last stop. They were all heading on up to Ottawa, had heard of my parents' inn, and several of them decided to stay there en route.

"In those days, of course, it was long trip from the St. Lawrence River to the capital; people drove mostly wagons and horses; there were very few automobiles, and they were always breaking down. People often got lost on the trip and had to turn back, especially in winter. As a result there was good business for the few inns along the route.

My father's was very popular because, despite his strictness with us, he was quite easy about his guests, accepting all classes and professions, so long as they were clean and not rowdy, and wouldn't drive away the businessmen he depended on for his everyday trade.

"That was quite a time. All of a sudden our inn was filled up, not with paunchy, benevolent travellers who talked about nothing but profits and loss and the weather, and sat after dinner snoozing by the fireplace, but with a strange assortment of artistes, who whistled and sang and danced about, juggled salt shakers, tied the serviettes in trick knots and joked obligingly with us girls, waving happily to our mother as she peered out with wary approval from the kitchen.

"I think those few days with the artistes and acrobats must have been the best of Thomas' life. He had loved the circus performance more than any of us, hardly touching the treats, but sitting open-mouthed at the antics of the clown and the trapeze artists. Now all these wondrous people suddenly appeared in our front parlour, sat on the veranda, wandered about the stables and the orchard, and what's more, they spoke to us, swung us about, called us by our names, and even allowed us to watch in awe as they fed raw meat to the sleepy, sinister panther.

"Thomas immediately became their favourite. You know, some people, then as now, see such performers almost as outcasts; they consider them not quite respectable, and treat them as marginal. Of course, the circus people always sense that, and in Thomas they found a kindred spirit, I suppose. They saw him, not as an unfortunate, but as a marginal person, as one specially gifted; indeed, as potentially one of their own. They assumed that he could take an active part in any little performance they improvised, that he could swing from a rope much better than us, guess where the rabbit was hidden, and read the panther's dark thoughts. They even suggested, almost seriously, that he might care to join them, and claimed they could train him to do everything they did, that he might indeed become a famous member of the troupe, and travel to many fascinating places all about the province and beyond. (Of course they never dared mention this to my mother and father).

"Finally, however, their stay had to end. They gave us a last dazzling little party. The clown, Rumford, could never have been funnier. Signor Giusto, the trapeze artist, stood on his head and did contortions. Signorina Giusto, his "sister", sang a song in Gypsy language about a talking bear. Monsieur Picadore, the ringmaster, imitated steam trains and whistles, while Georgina, the fat lady, passed around a special kind of chocolate that she said had come all the way from Europe: this was in the form of tiny, plump eggs, filled to bursting with delectable syrups that ran all over your tongue when you bit into them.

"Thomas, whose excitement was evident in the way he sprang about from guest to guest, and in his loud gasps of pleasure at every new trick, grew finally very sleepy. His head nodded, his eyes closed, and at last, well before midnight, father performed the ritual of carrying him up to bed. Mother followed, and tucked him in beneath his covers, but for once dispensed with the ritual bedtime story. A final farewell song sounded from his friends downstairs, who had gathered in the parlour, already seeming sad that they would have to leave early the next day.

"Still, the party did not lose its momentum. A second and third bottle of wine were opened; there was merriment but no real intoxication, and the circus people began to tell my mother how they loved and cherished Thomas. They said they could hardly bear to leave without seeing him at least once more, and so it was decided, with my parents' somewhat reluctant permission, that they would creep upstairs and bring him the very special present they had chosen for him: a small piece of frankincense, one they said had been carried all the way from Arabia and been blessed by some holy man whose name and denomination I forget now.

"It was a beautiful idea, we children thought, and we were very excited. Such rituals rarely happened in our household, and even if I was a bit jealous of all this attention bestowed on my younger brother, I wanted to see this final, very special show of that remarkable evening.

"We made our way slowly to the upper floor, our candles held carefully aloft and our steps very cautious despite the tittering and only half-suppressed jollity of the excursion.

"I remember the odd angled shadows, the sharp whispers, and little jocular phrases, some in French and Italian, as Jane and I led the Giustos, Rumford, Monsieur Picadore and the fat wobbling Georgina all the way to the third floor landing and to the door of that small attic room where our youngest lay sleeping under the roof and the stars.

"When we had all reached the threshold, jostling and joking with each other, I signaled that everyone should be quiet, then gently pushed open the door. We crept in quietly, all eight of us, the five adults and my sisters and I, and approached the small curtained bed, quite ready to make our secret night offering to my sleeping brother.

"The instant we pushed back the curtain, however, we were all struck motionless and silent.

"The room was a narrow well of darkness. One window, high up behind the dresser, gave a view of the night sky, and of the distant stars. The pinpointing lights of those stars appeared a faint white and yellow, but when I looked down at the bed and back again the outside illumination seemed to have vanished, so bright was the halo of light that surrounded the head of my brother.

"It was a blue shining circle we saw there, a gentle steady fire, as magical a light as in the old Bible pictures, the holy texts.

"We all stood gasping, or holding our breath. Then a low hushed murmur came from the performers, louder exclamations of wonder, and Signor Giusto actually made the sign of the cross, then shrank back and whispered, in a clear voice: *Santo Dio!*"

"My heart pounded with excitement, with terror, and I blinked fiercely to make the almost blinding light go away. But it didn't; it burned with a clearer and harder intensity, illuminating—with a strange kind of radiance—my brother's white forehead, his blond curls, his pure face. It was wondrous, but also a little frightening, and I just couldn't stand it.

"Without a word I ran from that suffocating little room. Downstairs, I found my parents sitting placidly before the fire and I babbled out a hasty, quite confused account of our strange discovery. Fortunately, the others appeared, practically on my heels, and confirmed what we had all seen, which our superstitious guests immediately declared to be a miracle.

"Our father and mother ran quickly upstairs and returned a few minutes later with puzzled, strained faces.

"'The boy is a saint, a holy one,' insisted Monsieur Picadore. 'I tell you, he must be taken as soon as possible to a priest. You English, alas, have no such miracles and your padre will understand nothing of this, but it is a miracle! I am so glad I have brought him the frankincense!'

"Madame Giorgina informed us that she had never seen a halo, except in holy pictures; she offered at once to buy from us something, any little thing, that Thomas had touched. It would be valuable, she explained; it might even work miraculous cures.

"All this, as I understand now, must have alarmed my sober and very Protestant parents, but they could not suppress the enthusiasm of the circus folk. Monsieur Picadore and the others sat for a long time around the fire, speaking in whispers. as if they were afraid to raise their voices, but their conversation was animated and full of an awestruck admiration. I have no doubt now, thinking back on that evening, that it must have been one the high points of all their circus journeys, perhaps of their lives.

"They left early the next morning, when both Thomas and I were fast asleep. I never heard any real news of the circus folk, and the incident of the boy's halo of light was never mentioned by our parents, though in our secret talk we three girls discussed many possibilities. My brother Robert, who had been out that night with his friends, had very little to say and reacted to his sisters' chatter with a shrug. Thomas seemed to know nothing of the striking event he had inspired."

****

"No, I've never told this story to anyone else," declared my grandmother—once again conversing with me directly—sipping a little water to soothe her throat after her long and somewhat emotional recital. I watched her gather strength for what came next, for I had heard vague stories and of course half-anticipated the sombre conclusion.

"Thomas was run over by a wagon the spring after that and died in the old Ottawa hospital without ever regaining consciousness," she informed me.

She told me this in a quiet voice, wiping her forehead with an old lace handkerchief that she kept under her pillow and helping herself to a little more water.

"So much for the notion of a miracle," she said, some bitterness in her voice now. "Oh yes, I had been jealous of that little boy, but I realized afterward how much I loved him. Despite what my parents said, I didn't believe any loving God could have cut him off like that.

"The whole thing just soured me so much on life that when I grew up I became the family skeptic. When I studied chemistry and psychology later (and I was the first one in our family to do so), I could see that that halo and vision we saw was all a matter of body heat and static electricity. So I didn't think any more about what manifestations might happen in the case of a boy like Thomas—or anyone else. I was sure that if it hadn't been for those superstitious circus folk, none of us would have taken the incident seriously at all, and maybe not even seen it."

My grandmother had no more to tell. Yet as I looked at her, high-minded, proud and indomitable, imprisoned by age and wealth inside those institutional coverlets, I wondered if her story was finished.

It's true, she herself never said any more to me about that night long ago in old Williamsburg, but it wasn't the last thing I heard about her involvement in it. After she died I discreetly questioned my mother, without actually revealing any details of Granny's strange vision, just because the old lady had made me swear not to.

"I could never stand your grandmother Martha's querulous ways, and all that God-mocking she liked to indulge in," said my mother.

"My father, poor man, endured it without complaining through a long life. *He* certainly went to church despite all that talk, and even forgave my mother her silly babble. He claimed she was really a very religious person. He said he had even seen visible signs of her goodness—I don't know what he meant by that—and he would never enlarge on the statement. But there were rumours, you know, that my mother on her sickbed had been visited by some kind of gift of light. I myself never saw anything and have no idea what that might have meant, although I spent more time with her than almost anyone.

"Then when she died suddenly and none of us could get to her in time, the nurses who had been with her dropped a few hints about what they'd seen, or thought they saw, on her deathbed. You were off at university, and I told them just to forget it, for who knows what these things mean?

"At any rate, she never changed, poor mother. She was a fanatic unbeliever until the end. While I never quite accepted it from her—all that harshness just seemed to be hiding something—I had no idea what she really thought about anything. There was also, I confess, something recalcitrant, something almost perverse, in her strong-mindedness—but there's no use me saying that, because I can see right away you won't understand such contradictions in a normal, useful person."

I didn't tell Mother, but the funny thing was, I thought I did.

Prime Time

Last night another woman invited me to go to bed with her. It happened in the bar of the Holiday Inn, and not only was I wearing clothes, but because of the bad spring weather I was sporting a raincoat, so it was a wonder she even recognized me.

"You're not offended, I hope," she added quickly. I shook my head and smiled at her composure.

She was quite a young thing, not a kid, but an early-twenties blonde in a dark jacket and tight jeans, and she swished the ice in her glass in a knowing fashion while I looked around, checking the escape routes.

But when I turned I couldn't help seeing in the mirror what a nice pair we made sitting there, she with her easy smile, her high cheekbones and dark-blue eyes, me with my young face, trimmed sideburns, and my shirt open just enough to show a patch of smooth chest.

"And you really are Chuck Daley?" she asked with a smile, shifting closer to my barstool but still glancing at me a little cautiously as if she expected me to deny it. I assured her that I was, and then she just upped and repeated the invitation.

I looked her over, grinned and said nothing. Possibly because I'm so jaded, I may even resemble the "very moral" man they write about in the gossip rags. Of course I took her proposition pretty much as a nice little ego booster for me and nothing else.

I loosened up and told her she was far too pretty to bother with me and if we ever did get together I hoped she'd have a studio paycheck waiting for her afterward. We had a good laugh over it, and I bought her a drink, and even took her telephone number. It wasn't impossible, I thought, that she could be a prospect, and they might actually want to look her over at some point, to take the nice wrapping off, so to speak, and see how her skin wore the light.

Of course I also had to run through my usual explanation (which happens to be quite true) that I don't do very many spontaneous liaisons, in bars or anywhere else. "I'm quite an old-fashioned guy," I told her, "I haven't bought into the fast-track lifestyle that seems to have hooked that whole new bunch of big names down at the studio. I know the guys are beginning to call me 'Mothballs,' and other pseudo-witty names. You realize—what did you say your name is?—oh yeah, Melissa—do you realize, Melissa, that the reviewers are beginning to write about the high percentage of reruns in my stuff? I'm confiding in you, now, you see.... Funny, huh? Most guys think shooting heavy scenes with nineteen-year-olds on the morning show, then spending the day getting stoned with starlets is cool. I think it's a pretty sad and limited way of life."

She gaped at me, wide-eyed, taking it all in.

"Of course they explain my antiquated ideas by the fact that I really have been around a long time, and because I came into my star status almost by accident."

I heard myself say that, then wondered whether she had read about it in one of the rag mags or seen one of my cheesy film bios. But it was soon clear that she was too bright by a long shot to bother with that kind of stuff. At about the third sentence she was on about the Marquis de Sade and Aleister Crowley, and she had an in-depth knowledge, it seemed, of the deep psychology of every female star who had gone the *Story of O* route, letting themselves be sadistically used by men, and enjoying it.

At that point I figured this girl was no grown-up groupie, but an ambitious kid who had caught a few shows and thought she'd like to get into the scene, even if it was only field-research for her Ph.D. on female masochism, male exhibitionism, or something equally non-piquant.

Using the mirror, I took a quick look around the bar. The place was quiet, really quiet, as only a fancy hotel bar can be on a rainy midweek night. There wasn't much chance that some snooping 'pappy' was going to appear to snap something to sell as an image of "the real me"—a shot that would eventually snake onto You Tube or land in some smudgy corner of a rag mag with a caption like: DALEY'S OFF WORK BUT NOT OFF HIS GAME. I didn't want any garbage like that, and you know how it goes these days. Everyone's on the make but always watching everyone else and wondering what kind of tricks they're doing in the family room in front of the TV, or upstairs in the soft lights of some hotel's specially soundproofed suites.

When I say I keep a low profile, I mean it. Publicity is fine, but it has to be properly staged. When they write that I really do have a nearly perfect body for a man of fifty-five, you can bet it's true. You can also bet I sweat my ass off in the gym four times a week and swim ten laps every morning before breakfast just to make sure it's true. I know that in our profession we have some cheaters (like the film porno bunch, who use stand-ins without so much as a credit) but I've never been guilty of that kind of hoax. None of us on TV do it; it's a matter of pride, or maybe just a professional code. I wouldn't want anyone out there to feel cheated. "That's Daley," the ladies say, especially the older ladies, "you know he never wanted to be a star like this. But he started it all, and he's the king."

By this time I sensed that the blonde didn't know much about the business really, but she was a likeable kid, so I decided to tell her my story, the famous story that many people know in outline but which very few have heard accurately from me. From the inside it resonates with some irony when it doesn't hurt—which is true for quite a few honest stories.

I suggested we go to a table and have a coffee and a cognac and after we'd settled down on either side of the fake table candles, I got to the point.

Twenty years ago it started, I told her. My God,

that's hard to believe, but the dates won't be argued with. I was another person back then, and yet in some ways just becoming myself. You know how it often works when you're young: a part of your personality, not always the nicest part, runs the show and the rest takes a holiday. Then all of a sudden comes the reckoning, life explodes in your face, and you drag what remains of yourself out of the wreckage and attempt to go on, with a different persona, a new face for the world...or else you don't.

I remember that winter very well, the weather was terrible, but things were going nicely for me. I'd had my syndicated column for nearly a year then, and was beginning to make some money. What's more, I was getting to be known as an acid-tongued but interesting panel guest, and regular interviewer on the local TV circuit. Whenever they wanted to rake some politico or special celebrity over the coals, they invited me on. I had a way of using those slots to raise the right questions, with just the right quantity of venom. I knew instinctively when to let up, when to let the poor squirming bastards off the hook, so they wouldn't hate me too much or refuse to talk to me again. The audience loved it, and my column was also selling around very well. It was beginning to be a good life. Lila and I had been married five years then, and things were going all right on that scene too.

I won't kid you, our relationship wasn't particularly exciting any more in the gut sense, but a pleasant enough routine had set in, and we had avoided all those big nasty rocks that lie in wait for most people's innocent little marriage boats. We had no children, and Lila worked as an editor for a New York publishing firm.

When I think back on it, she was a funny lady, old Lila, tall and gangly, with an odd high-pitched voice that under stress would pipe out exclamations or questions almost like a smart-assed five-year old. She was clever enough, and a liberal all the way (which was what attracted me to her in the first place), but when some example of political perfidy from the Right came to her attention, or if some other aspect of life—too raw and nasty to be assimilated— assaulted her mind, she'd act as if she'd just come out of a cave burial. She'd stand there goggle-eyed and her voice would pipe up suddenly, very shrill and excited. *"Oh my, can life really be this awful?"* she'd say. *"I just can't believe that people would do such things!"*

I could usually sympathize with her sentiments, but after a while her high-pitched little-girl outbursts made me wince. Occasionally she sang out in the same fashion during our bedtime frolics and it was all I could do to keep my focus on the main action. Luckily for my peace of mind, my day job involved a certain amount of legwork and quiet research, so we were used to doing a lot of things separately, and I didn't have to listen to her for more than a few hours out of twenty-four.

That was also fortunate because of her relationship with Jeff, a cute little Jack Russell terrier she'd been given by her layabout sister, a sibling who stayed with us much more than I'd have liked.

Lila was one of those women who can't do enough petting and fussing with any dog that happens to be at hand, and Jeff was always at hand. She talked to him incessantly, sometimes bursting out with little exclamations of pleasure at the wonderfully clever and loving things she claimed he did. (I tried to keep my wincing reactions hidden). Sure, I liked Jeff well enough, but I never fussed over him, whereas Lila and Jeff together were just poison.

There were a few other odd things about Lila, too trivial to mention, but some good and sweet things as well, so I have to say, although it may surprise you, that despite some temptation, until that winter I hadn't once been unfaithful to my wife. The same thing was true from her side too, I think, although you can never be quite sure about these things, can you? That winter did us in, though. Lila got saddled with a heavy assignment, having to get through a complete edit of a big manuscript before January, and she asked me to help her out. Could I please take over the dog-walking for a while? Normally Lila handled that, trotting out Jeff regularly at eight and five, if not more often. Jeff loved those walks, and always gave her an extra hand lick or two for her trouble.

For my part, although I'd learned to tolerate the little rat, I was a lazy son of a bitch when it came to routines other than my own, and if I took that dog for a walk three times in five years, I'd be surprised. Still, I gritted my teeth and accepted the job.

So every evening for a while I would give Jeff the signal and we'd go for a long hike through the rather posh neighborhood we lived in then, dodging the local poodles and always on the watch for all those damned pushy Dobes who'd been lured off their mats in front of the family safe to be given a little exercise and air.

Although I hate winter (which is one of the many reasons I live in California now), it wasn't a bad thing for me to do a little walking. In those days

I wasn't much into exercise and I'm sure all my trotting around that December did me a lot of good (Jeff flourished too, although he's been dead for a long time now.) The problem was that I always postponed those walks until the last possible time of night, sometimes until two or three in the morning, mostly because I was very busy writing, or monitoring some TV show for my column, but soon for another reason, one that changed my life altogether.

You have to remember that it was precisely at that time that the great TV revolution had begun, something people tend to attribute to my big breakthrough with Isobel, but of course that's rather inaccurate. I was talking to a very knowledgeable historian of popular culture the other day and he confirmed everything I've ever thought about this matter.

I'm sure you know exactly what I'm talking about. After the post-World War II era of the rating wars and the heyday of the sitcoms and talk shows, when the idiot tube seemed to threaten the movies, a kind of stagnation had set in. TV was in the doldrums. Why? There were many reasons, but the TV audience leveled off thanks to a rebound of big movies, and the increasing popularity of fast and uncensored live entertainments. TV bounced back with better sports and news coverage, and much later with many other things, right up to the onset of the "reality" shows. But by the time those arrived the whole computer revolution was in progress and the web, cell phones, and portable media of all kinds had pretty well killed the total dominance of the TV habit. There seemed no way to rebound from the challenge of all that new technology.

The powers that ruled the tube, however, still had a few tricks up their sleeves. The old networks had gone for "family entertainment," but with the arrival of specialty channels, and the tech revolution, the tepid, heavily censored "family" TV slowly disappeared and the revisioning started. It began with little shifts, like the shows based on action centers like police stations, hospital wards, and so on. Not to mention the violent crime shows, the cozy-violent British stuff, and the determination of some big networks to go out and film world events everywhere. Revolutions, riots, guerrilla wars, anything that would flare up—they had crews there before even the CIA could wink. Some people suggested that the companies actually started some of these things, just to get the footage, but of course that's never been proved. At the same time, they finally killed the censorship and the channels were flooded with X-rated movies, the more skin the better. And there were a lot of subtle changes, like the way people dressed, what they talked about, and what they could say on the shows.

For all the changes, though, nobody had dared to take the final step. Nobody had opened up the screen to real live sex, to daily hard-core broadcasts, or made a cult out of sex shows that featured regular stars. And that, my friends, is where Isobel's genius came in. To those that knew her, I guess, that wasn't much of a surprise. But my connection, my incredible role in all this—that was a surprise to everyone, and most of all, I guess, a surprise to me. As, of course, was Isobel, the inimitable one, who broke up my marriage and made me famous.

(At this point Melissa was riveted, so I bought her another drink).

I took a deep breath and explained to her that I'd first met Isobel at a small party, one I went to without Lila, lucky me. Isobel had just broken up with her latest partner, who was some kind of stock manipulator (later jailed), but she was well-known for founding the Gotham Art Center, which featured work of some of the great, famous moderns—de Kooning, Still, Motherwell, Kline, and so on. Isobel was originally from England, but she always looked vaguely Eastern European or Russian to me. She was even taller than Lila, had creamy white skin, slightly slanted eyes, and, needless to say, an absolutely ravishing body.

I spotted her right away at that party—that wasn't hard—and for some reason she seemed to latch onto me. She led me away into a corner and started talking to me about my show, and of course the first thing I noticed was her deep, sultry Lauren Bacall delivery, so different from poor Lila's high-pitched tremolo. She had me riveted in a minute, and of course I invited her to come on the show and talk about her art gallery and the artists she'd dealt with.

A few days later we made a spot for her and she did that. She was a terrific story-teller and it went very well, and I invited her to lunch and then dinner.

I quickly became obsessed with her, with her beauty, with the way she moved and smiled, with her surprisingly square name, her long-legged strong gait as she walked around our studio, and above all with her conversation. It was like none other I'd heard. When we met off the air, she had no reserve, it seemed, and nothing was off limits.

She told me how many men she'd slept with

(thirty-three at the time), laid out her views on sex—that our society was hopelessly repressed, that kids should be taught to masturbate, that group sex was the coming thing, that TV had to introduce full frontal nudity and live hard-core as soon as possible, that whoever did so would make a fortune. Needless to say, I was mesmerized.

The final push that sent me into the abyss was when she explained her special invention, a sex-game she asked all her newly acquired male friends to play with her. I sat bemused and dazzled while she explained the rules to me.

I won't go into the whole thing right now—I can send you all the details, if you're interested— but there was a complex erotic ritual that she'd created. It consisted of two people agreeing to certain mutual sexual acts. Each act had a point-value, and there were different levels of engagement. Level One was introductory and was mostly sex-at-a-distance; the next levels consisted of direct contact, intensifying bit by bit. I can only give you a few examples right now—not that I've forgotten any of them! But in brief, at Level One you would do things such as masturbate at a mutually agreed-upon time, while the other person (who was somewhere else) would meditate on your experience, Or one person would clip off a bit of public hair and wear it in their pants or panties all day. Or a player would write a description of being dominated and compelled by a lover in ways he or she found exciting, then at the next meeting would read it to the other player. Things like that! All kinds of exciting things that she very creatively devised for us to do apart and together!

So the games began, and we played them right through Level One, and pretty soon reached Level Two, when we actually got into much more serious sex, sex that was more exciting than anything I'd ever done, heard of, or dreamed about. All this, through a month or two that flew by in a crazy blur of secret meetings, early evening motel stops, house calls (she lived close by), clandestine sleepovers, frantic afternoon lay-bys, or dangerous moments in public halls, parks, or parking lots.

Meanwhile, in my saner—and much duller— moments, I carried on with Lila, who didn't seem to notice a thing but continued piping down her own very tame valleys of virtue and simplicity and hard work. It was sad, but what could I do? I was absolutely crazy for Isobel.

That's how it was, and just after it began, I started those walks with our dog Jeff that I mentioned earlier. At first this was a dream situation, since I had a ready excuse to go out of the house at almost any moment of the day or night. Poor Jeff spent a lot of time waiting for me while I worked my way up on the pleasure scale, moving from Isobel's Level One to Level Two. Soon, though, the waits became too long, too awkward, and I hired a neighbour's kid to take over most of the walking, explaining to Lila that I was getting just too busy to find the time every day or night.

But no sooner had I done that than things between Isobel and me changed a little; we seemed to go from the first frantic phase to something different, something cooler, more distant, more self-conscious.

I began to be more alert to her, to see little details I had ignored before: the way her eyes shifted oddly when she didn't want to hear something, the way she tossed her head and licked slightly at her lips when she grew excited. I noticed how much more stringent, almost masculine, her dress was, and how her hairstyle and makeup changed, becoming more formal on days when she was the most distant and preoccupied, days that become more frequent after the first frantic weeks of our liaison.

At that point I began to grow a little nervous,

wondering whether she was getting tired of me. I was so hooked on her by then that I was naïve enough to think—as many would have done—that the very behaviour that had attracted me in the first place would change as we grew closer, that now that we had become familiar lovers, the games would wither away, and she would be tamed and more ready to fall in with my more reserved and regular ways.

I didn't at first see the obvious: that she was just being herself, looking, perhaps unconsciously, for a new conquest, and that it would soon be time for her to move on to partner number thirty-five in her erotically structured game of life.

Then, on one of those winter nights, the truth suddenly dawned on me, and I panicked. With a terrible clarity I saw that from the first her game must have been to make me fall in love with her, and become helplessly attached. That she'd continued to play out the elaborate rituals of love—her way of combining pleasure and power—while remaining quite uninvolved with me in any deeper sense. I had become her love puppet and now she was preparing to drop me.

I stood still in my elegant little home office, my computer running on and then suddenly winking into the screen saver I had so cleverly chosen for it.

Big bold letters that seemed now to mock me and my absurd dreams of love:

THEY WENT TO SEA IN A SIEVE THEY DID, IN A SIEVE THEY WENT TO SEA. IN SPITE OF ALL THEIR FRIENDS COULD SAY. ON A WINTER'S MORN, ON A STORMY DAY...IN A SIEVE THEY WENT TO SEA...

I was frantic, terrified, suddenly afraid of losing her. My life seemed to be collapsing around me. I had to see her that moment. To talk, to try to engage her love, her feelings, the tenderness I knew must be there, behind the endless charades and scripts. And now, although we always planned our meetings quite carefully, and were seldom spontaneous, things were in crisis. I simply couldn't wait.

It was still just before midnight. Lila, I knew, had already gone to bed exhausted. So I got on the phone and cancelled the dog walker I sometimes used, and who'd agreed to come late that night. (I didn't dare call Isobel, for fear she might put me off). Within minutes, I had hitched up old Jeff and we were heading in her direction.

It was cold and I was glad she didn't live very far away. I walked between the silent houses, and down the small private lanes that sliced across the big back yards. The wind came out of the shadows to chill me, and I found myself commiserating with Jeff, although he appeared to be in a state of extreme delight. After a few blocks we came around by one of the newer developments, a little warren of high status mews, English style, that some contractor had plunked down in the middle of the neighborhood. She had recently moved there.

As I walked along the snow-edged streets, shivering a little in the cold, my heart beating fast, I began to remember many of the things I'd heard about my Isobel, rumors I must have picked up and ignored or immediately dismissed, conversations that had been forced on me, things I had overheard, allusions to her that only days before I had found absurd.

It seems that my dazzling Isobel had quite a reputation, not so much as a lover, but as a social climber and operator, She had come in from the west coast to open her gallery in New York and in order to become a reigning princess of the arts scene, had stepped over a whole lot of bodies, male and female. She had made huge profits, often at the expense of her lesser artists. She was reputed to be money-hungry, ruthless, to have connections with unsavoury characters, perhaps the mob, and—although some of her victims might have had an interest in doing so—nobody had been able to expose much of her private life.

All such gossip, and more, I had dismissed, and even laughed at. I thought of her quite differently— as a brilliantly creative explorer, a love-partner out of my dreams, somebody I could settle down with for life. I had been entranced and bedazzled, but thought myself cool and self-confident, until tonight that is. Now here was Jeff, who knew the way only too well, pulling at the leash, tugging me toward my destiny in the elegant mews across the park where I had already gone through such rituals of pleasure and pain.

You have to keep in mind how these houses are designed. They feature floor to ceiling glass, giving views down the lanes and across the tailored lawns, and there's not much reason to cover everything with curtains in that kind of neighborhood, at least downstairs.

I stole across the park like a thief. A few cars rolled past; I could see a couple of other dog-walkers near the main boulevard. But the wide green in front of her walkway was empty, as were the small benches set here and there between the entrances; the only movement was some shifting light on the snow-sprinkled greensward cast by figures that flitted around inside the apartments.

I walked on, afraid that she might be out somewhere, *with someone,* and at the same time I was fearful of how she'd react if I found her at home. My steps made a squishy unpleasant sound on the snow-soaked grass as I crossed over to her walkway. Then I looked up at her house and suddenly saw her.

I stopped in my tracks. Jeff turned and whined softly, tugging at the leash.

I looked through the big front window, and saw her standing on the bottom steps of a long staircase, a few feet from her front door, She seemed to be doing something with a large painting because she was holding a huge canvas in her hands, gazing pensively around as if she were about to place the thing somewhere on her glaring white walls.

She looked elegant and quite untouchable, wearing a clinging green negligée kind of thing, her dark hair gleaming in the light. I watched as she suddenly put down the painting, resting it on the stairs, then moved down the steps, disappearing for a moment, and finally coming back into sight, the white bone of a telephone in her hand.

She sat on the bottom steps, beside the painting, talking on the phone, smiling and nodding.

I stepped back into the shadows and watched her

in complete fascination, after a while even forgetting my nervous fear that somebody would come along and nail me as the neighborhood voyeur.

With her head resting lightly on the banister, she chatted into the phone, her lips purling into camera smiles, her free hand pointing gestures in the air.

Fascinated, I gradually edged my way closer, holding Jeff on the leash against his natural impulse to continue our interesting walk.

I could see the white line of her neck, her legs crossed under the gown, the silver points of her slippers like tiny fish darting in a bowl of light. Looking both right and left, I moved under the skimpy branches of a developer's tree. She stood up with a toss of her head, her back toward me, and my glance ran up the seams of her gown. Suddenly, she turned. I ducked and stepped forward—into emptiness. I bumped into a bench I hadn't noticed and fell, clutching Jeff's leash.

Jeff started to bark and pulled with a wild tugging strength at the leash. A rabbit shot away across the lawn and disappeared. I lay in a snow patch, assaulted by shrill volleys of barking.

Struggling to recover, I tangled the leash on the bench, as Jeff began to howl much louder. The sharp click of a lock and I found myself wriggling foolishly across a patch of brilliant light. I caught a glimpse of my princess's door, flung open, and saw her standing there peering out at me.

"What's going on?" she called, in her all-too-familiar voice.

The door slammed, but just as I finally got the leash untangled and bullied Jeff into silence, her door opened again. She was wearing some kind of heavy fleece and coming toward me down the path.

"It's you! I should have known. What in hell are you doing here at this time? And crawling across the lawn. We were scheduled for Thursday, weren't we?""

She came a bit closer. I looked up into the angry eyes of my princess, my mind grabbing my tongue and trying to make it work. Half into a stammered excuse, I saw her expression soften, as I slowly pulled myself to my feet.

"I won't make any jokes about your dropping in," she said, "but it's a really bad time. I was on the phone and I have to deal with something urgent. Are you OK? I thought you were coming over on Thursday? Or is there a problem?"

Her distant manner made me ashamed of my weakness. I tried to conceal my desperation, thinking, *I don't care if she chastises me, I'm just glad to see her in the flesh.* But I hid my desperation.

"Sorry," I said. "Jeff here dragged me in this direction, and then a rabbit scurried away and frightened him, and he tripped me up. I was just passing by."

She gave me a doubtful look, standing there shivering in the cold air. Her body moved underneath her thin gown and I winced a little, seeing her so distant, indifferent. Then some demon of jealousy prompted me to add in a touchy voice: *"I didn't mean to interrupt anything private. You can get the hell right back to your interesting conversation."*

"What? Oh, God, Chuck! You were spying on me! Well, spare me the innuendo. As a matter of fact I was setting up something with a technician, but it wasn't a private call. Pull yourself together, for God's sake! You *are* coming over on Thursday?"

I was ashamed, mortified. I said of course I would come. She leaned over, hugged me, kissed me and stroked my cheeks. Her nose was cold, her hands wet, but it felt spontaneous, sincere. I wanted her badly—it seemed in those days I always wanted her. But she stood back and smiled, and said goodbye.

She walked a few steps back toward her building, but stopped suddenly, turned to me and said: *"It's Level Two, number twenty-five. Don't you forget! I'm looking forward to it."*

She wasn't referring to the building of course, but to the key number of our sex game. In the last few days I'd lost track of the sequences, and didn't know which of her carnal inventions she was referring to. I couldn't wait to get home to find out.

Her door closed, and I stood there a minute, both dazzled and shaken, until Jeff began his infernal barking again. I danced him away with mixed curses and blessings and made my way home in a zigzag of profound confusion.

The next day I mooned around the house, unable to do any work. I called the kid and set up Jeff's walks for the day. Then I took Isobel's list of games from a locked desk drawer and settled down in a frenzy of wild imaginings, to read my Thursday's fate.

Wednesday rolled past slowly. Lila wanted to go out to dinner, so we did. I watched her across the table, irritated by her girlish foppery and foolish bonhomie. But I covered my disapproval by showering her with compliments and pretending to be fascinated by her latest discovery of the perfidy of the Right. I thought: *what a boring manner she has; how could I have married someone so lacking in sexual drive and interest? How could I ever have*

*been turned on by her flat-chested, skinny body?
And that voice! Oh my God!*

When we got home I delayed retiring to our bed in
case one of her infrequent urges toward sex should
occur. I couldn't have stood her body next to mine
that night. I thought with real joy that I would be in
Isobel's arms the next morning.

Thursday I saw to it that Jeff got his walk early.
I gave him an extra ration of food and slipped out,
leaving him chomping contentedly in the kitchen.
The cold air in my face couldn't calm me down
much, but I was careful of my footing and arrived
at Isobel's upright and on time. I had spent the
morning poring over the text of our scheduled sex
game, so I was more than ready.

Isobel had set it all down in her own handwriting.
I won't go into all the details, but for this meeting
she had specified that everything take place in her
large, mostly empty, exercise room, that I be bound
up and assaulted, then at some point I would break
my bonds, pursue her around the room, playing
hide and seek for a while, using a few convenient
shoji screens, then finally consummate everything
on a huge divan she had obtained from a harem
somewhere in the East.

It sounded like a nice morning's work, and just

thinking about it made me stiff and excited.

The door was unlocked. I locked it behind me and went into the big downstairs reception room with its curving staircase and fancy chandelier.

She met me wearing a white dress through which I could faintly see the outline of her Gauguin yellow bra and panties. We kissed for a long time, and she led me upstairs. As usual, there was no drink and no small talk, hardly a greeting. Those were the rules.

We went straight to the exercise room, a place I barely remembered, a big high-ceilinged space with very bright recessed lights illuminating the white-tiled floor. I remembered thinking that the place looked like a studio, but I was too distracted by the white operating table, centrally placed, the leather straps, the whip, the big divan, and a few other suggestive accoutrements to pursue any very complex thoughts.

Isobel, or what might have been her wraith-like semblance, all white and impassive, pointed me to the shoji screens near the far wall. Behind them I found a short white robe and a pair of oddly-tinted goggles, which I knew I was meant to put on. When I did so, after stripping down and donning the robe, the room took on a violet hue and the space around me shimmered slightly, as if with the beams of some hidden magic light.

I looked around, a little dazzled already, and saw a small white table close by. On it sat a single clear glass half full of a green tinted liquid. I knew I was meant to drink this and I obediently did so.

Then I sat down in the white cane chair beside the table and waited.

Within minutes, my whole body relaxed. I felt weightless, as if I might float away, and everything—the screens beside me, the table, the empty glass, the walls a few feet away—gave me a glad feeling as I looked at them. Their secret essence seemed suddenly revealed, and I found them consoling, meaningful, reassuring.

Time passed—it might have been a few minutes, or a few hours, and then a screen moved. Isobel, or a woman who in another dimension was Isobel, had moved it. She stood there, holding the whip I had seen earlier, clasped loosely in her left hand. She was dressed in a long white gown that revealed all the contours of her body, but her eyes were slightly hidden by a small white mask. She looked at me; I felt her scorn, her indifference, her superior power, then she made a slight gesture with the whip, and I moved to the center of the room, slipped out of my robe, and kneeled beside the table....

Once again, time seemed endless, but irrelevant. She used the whip lightly, but I was totally in her power and soon bound up, strapped to the white table.

She did as she wished with me. The whole scenario played out. Her dominance continued for a long time, but finally—as the script required—I broke out of my spell and resisted. I gained power and subdued her. She had ridden me at her will, but in the end I lay atop her and brought her screaming to a climax on the big divan.

We lay exhausted for a long time. Champagne seemed to magically appear on the small table behind the shoji screen. We refreshed ourselves and played out another long sequence, one that involved a kind of inspired hide and seek, and also ended in an explosive climax, this one mine.

The game was finally over. What she felt I don't know, but I found myself elated, exhausted, transformed, happier than I had ever been, but with that familiar slight emptiness that usually follows on such frolics.

We said almost nothing, but drifted downstairs, reassembling ourselves slowly, as if it had all been a dream. We had a drink together. I asked her about the strange room, but she didn't want to discuss it.

"Let's not spoil perfection with small talk," she said. "I think that you should dress and go now. I'll get in touch with you very soon."

I started to protest, very gently, but she was not to be moved. "You'll have to do as I tell you," she said quietly, giving me a look.

I went away, my whole body aglow. I thought of her constantly until we met again, the next night. And once again she insisted we make love in that bare white room, although the scenario was very different.

"You've got some kind of purity hang-up," I joked with her, but she didn't any longer want to discuss our games, or much of anything, it seemed.

We went on like this for a full week, skipping the odd night, and with constantly changing encounters.. She was always cool and distant, but gave me more than I had ever dreamed possible in a sexual encounter, and I thought how unjust those gossips were who described her as ruthless and selfish. Her generosity did come, however, with an aloofness and reserve that made it ten times more compelling. I would have killed for the woman.

I was expecting her next to announce a change of scenario, or to propose that we move on to another level of the game. Secretly, I thought the games would lead smoothly into something quite different, that our connection would transpose into something more personal and committed, but still rare, into a married love that was both totally sensual and thoroughly mystical and strange. Of course I wanted us to live together. It seemed impossible that we could ever part after such intimacies. I knew I simply *had* to live with her, because I couldn't imagine being deprived of her for more than a few hours. I was addicted.

Sadly, it didn't quite happen as I'd hoped.

One day (it was the following Monday, in fact) I got a phone call from my lawyer. He wanted me to come to his office right away, but he wouldn't tell me any more about it.

Of course I was sure Lila had found out about the affair and was coming after me. All my guilt started up and I trailed along to see the lawyer, feeling confused and suddenly weary. At the same time I was happy that things would be resolved at last, that I was about to escape my imprisoning marriage, that I could begin to share my life with the woman without whom I couldn't imagine being alive at all.

When I got to the lawyer's office, he was with

another client. I sat there, thinking how I wanted to call Isobel and talk this over with her. I knew I would have to leave Lila, there was no way I could give up what I had with my power woman, my sensual darling.

My lawyer's name was Harris, a bright young man not long out of law school. He was a very meticulous fellow who always wore a fresh white carnation in his lapel. I had trouble believing that he stood up before the judges like that, but maybe with his clients he wanted to strike a certain note. Since he was otherwise as soberly pinstriped as an old-fashioned undertaker, who cared? I laughed to myself, thinking how shocked the foppish bastard would be if he knew about my love games with Isobel.

The cheery receptionist finally ushered me in to his over-tidy inner sanctum. Harris shook hands and smiled a bit sourly. He seemed rather nonplussed as he handed me a note and pointed to a small table on which I saw a black metal case.

I looked at the note. It wasn't from Lila at all; it was from Isobel and it read as follows:

Dear Chuck,
Please take the film I've sent to you down to the

studio and run it through. Look at it by yourself,
please, and give me a call when you're finished.

As ever, Isobel

"A Ms. Mercer rang," Harris told me. "Isobel Mercer. She sent over that box containing a film, together with some papers that she thought you might want to discuss with me. I haven't opened them because she insisted that you watch the film first. This is a rather awkward business, it seems. What's going on?"

I shrugged my shoulders. "I have no idea. It's a private matter for sure. I don't have any business with this lady. What should I do, I wonder?"

"Why don't you just ask her what's up?"

"Can I use your phone?"

He pointed to the desk. I rang Isobel but there wasn't any answer.

I decided that there must be some reason for the strangeness of all this, but I was suddenly frightened, I'm not sure why. Hopefully it wasn't some set-up to sue me for rape, or some trick or plot of the innocent Lila to catch me out?

Harris insisted that he knew nothing. The message and canister had come by hand. Of course you can imagine what happened then. I went to the studio and did get a room set up. I started the film running, and sat there in dark for a full ten minutes before I could move my hand over to shut it off. What I had seen by then of the white room, of our bodies, of the passion that was so real that no acting could ever match it had made me sick.

I sat there for a while in that sickness of mind and I wondered what was happening to me. I turned the film on again, shaking with anger. I watched the charades playing out. The white room, the shoji screens, the divan, the white table. The bodies moving together and apart and the ecstatic dance toward consummation.

Only after the anger had wrenched me and changed me did I admit to myself that I was enjoying what I saw there, that I was riveted by it, totally turned on by what I saw. Only after a longer time in that dark room did it strike me that I had seen two strangers playing out a script that was shocking, yet both beautiful and complete.

I ran the film over and over. I stopped frames where it gave me pleasure. I wanted to do nothing so much as to make love to Isobel Mercer again before that camera.

I packed up the film and went to the Greek bar near my home. I called Isobel. After ten or twelve rings she came on the line. The sound of her voice started the pictures again, in my mind. My voice cracked as I spoke to her, begging her to come away with me, telling her how much I wanted to see her again, to make love. We could make love while her film was running, on that very same white floor.

She was silent, and halfway through a sentence I thought of Harris and questioned her:

"You want to use the film to scare off Lila? But you don't need to! And why send it to Harris? He's a Puritan—he's...irrelevant!"

She laughed quietly and started to break the news to me. "Chuck, he's not irrelevant. He's going to draw up the agreement between us and oversee the network contract. I've checked him out. You've got the right guy. He'll do a good job."

"*The network contract*? What the hell are you talking about?"

It was then she started to fill me in on the plan, her grand design to make television history. She had already got excited interest from the Mutual Network in a show that would go the limit, a show that would feature regular broadcasts of virtuoso love-making, tasteful, beautiful, hugely erotic. She had pitched her idea very well and the network had been keen enough to jump in with all their technology for a trial: they had provided technicians and done a complete makeover of her house. They were convinced that they had something explosive. It would be a calculated breakthrough, carefully organized, and would challenge the public to deal with the ultimate sexual experience as a new feature of home viewing.

She went on, but the phone slipped out of my hand and struck against the upholstered wall of the restaurant. It swung there a minute and then I retrieved it and listened.

She was still talking, explaining how she had planned this with someone else but had decided on me on a whim when we finally got together and she had tested me sufficiently. She hadn't confided in me because she liked the idea of spontaneity on the part of her performers, and she didn't trust me "to have the balls" to take it on.

"This isn't going to happen, Isobel." I took a deep breath and tried hard to reign in my anger. I wanted to kill her, but she wasn't within reach, and I knew my anger would fail by the time I could confront her. I knew she'd have everything worked out, that I was in her power, that I half wanted to be, and that my only misery was the certain knowledge that I would never again make love to her with the innocence and joyful depravity I had felt up to now in her arms.

"Be sensible, Chuck," she went on to advise me. "If you refuse to sign the papers Lila gets the tape. If you sign, you almost certainly become an instant star and a millionaire to boot. If you really want that floppy doll you can buy her off, you know. Women hang around longer when their errant husbands get rich, and if she leaves and it costs you, so what? You'll make it back in a few months. I expect you to be a regular on my new show. Making love to beautiful women and drawing a big paycheck for it. Not bad, don't you think?"

"To turn myself into a male whore?"

"That's melodramatic, for God's sake, and just plain inaccurate. Your lawyer has the papers in a sealed envelope. If you're not satisfied with the deal, work it out with him. And don't worry about federal regulators or anyone like that; everyone will be bought off. C'mon—you'd be a fool not to dive in. We'll talk again when you cool down."

She hung up then, abruptly, and of course there was no sign of tenderness, no words of affection, no mention of thanks. Her love-making had been purposeful and business-like and now that the business deal was in view, and ready to be concluded, every pretense of emotion could be dropped.

Isobel thought it was better that we not see each other for a while. But if I decided I wanted to be a part of it, all I had to do was sign the contract. Of course there was no point in me trying to claim damages of any kind, nor could I stop the show, because they would fight me and win; they had plenty of money.

I guess I don't have to tell you how it took me. I wanted to kill her, but there isn't any violence in me. I wanted to make love to her, but she wouldn't see me privately at all. Finally, I got tired of calling, of watching for her on the streets and never having the courage to face her; and I didn't want to think about the string of new lovers I suspected she'd soon take on.

The show ran and you know the rest. The series went into orbit. It was a sensation. Our first white-room session wouldn't seem very daring to anyone now, we've gone so much further in style and technique, but it retains a great deal of charm, I hear, for the people who run it at the DVD clubs, and it's still earning me a lot of money: Isobel was very scrupulous about the financial arrangements. Most people have read in the gossip columns how Lila divorced me soon after I started my career, how

Isobel died of an overdose a few years later, rich from many sources, including the publication of her book on sexual games, but broken-hearted over some football or hockey player. I guess that showed she had a heart after all.

Of course that's all history now, with a touch of the comic. The dog, for example. After Jeff died, someone bought his carcass, stuffed it and gave it to some animal actors' museum. And he'd never even been on screen in any of our shows.

But as you well know, the shows continue. And tastes keep changing all the time. Who knows where it will go from here? But it all started in that blank white room of long ago, or pretty nearly.

And as to that famous little sex drama, I have a funny take on that sometimes. I cast my mind back to what I experienced there and I somehow delude myself into thinking that maybe neither one of us was acting. I know I wasn't, and of course I have no excuse for my naïve, stupid passion, nor any guilt about getting sentimental over Isobel. Self-protection maybe? Not wanting to seem the complete fool?

****

So that was it. I'd finished my story. Melissa was still there, across that table in one corner of that bar in the Holiday Inn.

She had listened very attentively and now she was looking at me with some amazement and maybe quite a bit of sympathy, or even a touch of pity. (I hope I'm imagining the latter).

I sat back, staring down at the eternally-burning fake candles, and smiled my nicest fake smile at my beautiful listener. I realized that I didn't know how to read her; I'm very poor at reading women, even now. Maybe she was nothing but a grownup groupie after all. Even so, it was late. I thought (and had been thinking all through my story) that maybe it was time I took a step in a different direction. I invited the beautiful Melissa upstairs. I didn't see any photographers or hidden cameras, but she turned out to be even lovelier in bed than I had imagined.

My studio will give her a trial, if she wants one, on my recommendation. When I mentioned it, she seemed to be interested, so I guess that's maybe what she was after all the time. You might take this as another example of just what an old-fashioned guy I am, or what kind of a sucker I can be.

But when you buy or rent my first classic, "The White Room," and see that long lithe body pounding against mine, in colour, in slow motion, in replays that bring out every nuance of style and of skill, you'll forget about that, about any deficiencies of character or plot.

You may even realize what kind of talent it's taken for me to make it, all these years, in prime time.

Brindisi: *Libiamo!*

You must know *La Traviata*, that wonderful Verdi opera. What lilting heartbreak, what a tuneful tragedy!

It was one of Louise's favourites, she who had begun by mistaking *The Phantom of the Opera* for the real thing. But give her credit: Louise was a fast learner, brisk and efficient in action—except when she had some devilish and complex social plot in progress; then she would slow down and enjoy each moment, watching her venom act on her helpless victims. Always queenly of mien, however, she worked from on high, true to her stately self-image, even in the most cruel of her manipulations.

Take her recent birthday party for Anna, intended

to celebrate her old friend's fortieth. Louise had a real vision for that one, and masterminded everything, only prodding her husband, David, to take over the arrangements when one of her patients had a crisis. (It will not surprise you that she, the least self-understood and most self-centred woman of anyone's acquaintance, should be a psychologist and social counsellor.)

Dolores and Jeff were invited to the party, of course, as was Anna's husband, Neil. Everybody knew everybody from long ago, which was both a good thing and a dangerous thing.

Poor David was ordered to book a private setting, for preference the Papineau Room in Le Scandale, a trendy west-end French restaurant that all three couples frequented. If Louise was busy just then, so was David: busy losing money. Week by week, day by day, his bookstore was going under. It was a New Age place—Zen, tarot, Deepak Chopra, and yoga— but the incense and the noodling music were no match for the smell of coffee, the discount prices, the bump of real contact in the places down the street. The old auras were dissipating, the myths were leaking away. When David greeted his few remaining regulars, they didn't know it, but he wasn't waving, he was drowning.

He was no fool, though, and the accountant he used was a distant cousin, so to keep things afloat they did a few tricks with the bookkeeping. It was cleverly organized, but David made a bad mistake: he told Louise all about it. Her consulting room was on the second floor, right above his bookstore, and there was no hiding anything from her. She had been married once before, to Jack; he had betrayed her, discreetly, but when it all came out it was a real tangle, with some of her closest friends involved and her bank account plundered. Despite his New Age trappings, David was closely watched; this KGB role suited Louise, since she was a born snooper, and totally lacking in self-doubt.

David, of course, was eager to please Anna. Most men were. She was still a beauty, with lovely curves and a model's face, if also a sharp serpent's tongue. Years ago, when she'd been a student at the university where he lectured, she had walked once past Neil's open office door. From that moment on he was mad about her. Neil was something of an expert on criminology and deviant behaviour, but after sleeping with her he found that when he looked in the mirror all his professional cool deserted him. He was simply Jekyll gazing at Hyde, and he knew that the Wolf Man lurked behind his bleary, goddess-dazzled eyes. Most of the time he stayed coherent, remembered to brush his teeth and tie his shoelaces, but the very thought of her blonde voluptuous nakedness sent him raving, and after they ran away together he suffered much insecurity. There was suspicion and jealousy, drunken pursuits of other women as a compensation, and dishes flying around the kitchen.

Anna was both intrigued and frustrated by her newfound professor. He was quite a bit older than she was and often seemed out of touch with the then exciting present—that hangover period after the great era of 1960s rock concerts, nose-thumbing at authority, and casual sex. When Neil and Anna had been married for the mystical seven years, she got restless. They were living in no great style in the country, and while working at a boring job in the city she became fascinated with a slim, handsome oriental karate instructor, a Bruce Lee without portfolio. Unfortunately for her peace of mind, she was a sleepwalker, and during one evening's ramble she blurted out her lover's name. Neil, a typical husband, didn't at first catch on, but she finally confessed all. Whereupon he drank almost all of a bottle of rum and went after her with a kitchen knife. She survived without a scratch, but he jumped out of a second-floor window and ended up on crutches. She retreated to the west coast and took up with a doting Stanford physicist.

It was, in other words, a typical love-match, which—after the physicist was dumped, and Neil threw away his crutches—resumed, with slightly different rules.

Dolores and Jeff, Louise's other friends, were a different case. Dolores had a bohemian background—of sorts. Her paternal grandparents had been the last of a long line of Jewish art dealers. They had lived in Paris long ago, mixing with the likes of Hemingway, Henry Miller, and Man Ray. Her parents, though, became a squabbling stockbroker family, and they eventually settled in Montreal.

Depressed from childhood, Dolores decided to study psychology, and in graduate school at McGill met Jeff, a doctor's son, well brought up, slim, dark-browed, silent, and seemingly intense. They married, and Dolores quickly acquired an array of sedatives that kept her comatose enough to be forgiven for her constant inertia. Jeff's intensity, on the other hand, turned out to be the all-too-visible struggle of a deeply repressed man not quite able to ventriloquize his inner child. Their sole offspring, Cassandra, was quickly ensconced as one half of a pretty sticky father-daughter duo, with Dolores playing the all-embracing mother. That pampered young Cassie was destined for trouble later on.

Just before the west-end soirée, Jeff had fallen in love with a beautiful woman, who turned out to be a transgender butterfly. Dolores forgave him, but it did shake her confidence in both his instincts and his perceptions. It never occurred to her to do anything about it, however, and Jeff began to see the advantage of having a consistently tranquilized wife.

Unlike her beautiful but obviously addicted old friend, Louise had achieved that state of perfection that brooks no dissent and suffers no criticism. Everything she did, however limited, unsuccessful, or unpleasant, was cast in the spotlight of her own rapturous gaze. "There I go!" her every gesture boasted. "Here I am!" was the subtext of her every sentence. She displayed her virtues to others with the wonderful assurance that in doing so she was bestowing on them a favour, unique and treasurable. When they were unappreciative—which was often—she was properly scornful.

Her running commentary on her husband's inadequacies was, of course, unrelenting, trivial, and wearisome.

"David isn't interested in sex."

"David doesn't know how to handle money."

"David always overcooks the asparagus."

After a while this hectoring—and David's silences or inadequate, half-mumbled responses—woke the slumberous Dolores from her doldrums. She took on the role of David's defender. Louise struck back, and a gap widened between the two erstwhile psychology students.

"Dolores is a congenital depressant," Louise would confide to Anna. "I knew she'd never get her Ph.D. She sits around all day waiting for Jeff to say something, then she contradicts him. Cassandra is Daddy's girl; she dotes on Jeff. When Dolores tells her what to do, she just laughs."

In her non-combative moments with Dolores, Louise would talk about Anna. "She's smart enough," Louise would concede, "but of course she's got no discipline. She throws around shrink terms, almost all from Jung, but she doesn't know much about any real psychology. She dropped out of nursing and fell into teaching. Not like you and me, Dorry; we're professionals."

Dolores would disagree and try to qualify, then Louise would subtly change the subject. "I don't know if your Cassie will ever get over her Daddy hang-up. It must make it hard for her to relate to boys."

"All the boys have crushes on her," Dolores would say. "She's very popular."

"Is that what she tells you? She's probably trying to make Jeff jealous. It's a shame she's so passive."

"I don't think she's passive. And that's not true about Jeff!"

"You're her mother, Dolores. You wouldn't see it."

The day of the great birthday party arrived. David had done exactly as he was told, and had booked the elegant chambre séparée. The night before, however, Louise called Anna and confided that this would be the last joint celebration for her and David: she was going to file for a divorce. She hadn't told David yet; she didn't want to spoil the evening for him. Besides, she wanted to get a head start with her lawyer. David wouldn't stand a chance anyway, since she knew all his dirty bookkeeping secrets.

"That seems a pretty rotten way to start divorce negotiations," Anna told her.

"I don't agree. I was just talking to Dolores. Naturally she sided with David. What's the matter with that woman? Can't she see what a slouch David is? He'll soon be bankrupt and then he'll drag us both down. And Anna, he just won't give up smoking! How can any sane man smoke in this day and age? I'm insisting that he sleep at the store from now on. Maybe he'll take the hint?"

The conversation dragged on, with Louise doing most of the talking. Anna felt more and more irritated. She had recently given up smoking and now she herself longed for a cigarette. Just the fact that Louise disapproved of smoking made it more attractive. At the same time, she had lost most of her respect for David. How could a man let this bitch kick him around?

"I hope you don't go through with this," she said, trying to be diplomatic. "You've both worked so hard at your marriage."

"I've worked hard, you mean! David doesn't know the meaning of work."

Getting ready for the dinner the next day, Anna and Neil got into one of their running disputes. It started out when she asked him if he liked her dress.

He hesitated—this was dangerous territory—then took a shot at it.

"It looks nice but it's...a little buttoned up."

"What do you want, a plunging neckline?"

"Sure, that would be great. What about that

wonderful Victoria's Secret dress I just bought you?"

"Are you crazy? I'm not wearing that. I'm not twenty years old any more!"

"That's a shame, but the dress looks good on you anyway."

"You just want me to show flesh. It flatters you."

"It doesn't flatter me. I married you for your mind, not your body."

"Oh my God! Tell me another!"

When Anna had found a suitable dress—a retro navy blue cotton, with white boarding-school collar and cuffs—they climbed into the car and attempted to take off. By this time they were arguing about money.

Unfortunately, their old battered Volvo coughed a little on starting, then died altogether. It was a perpetual trial to them.

"See what I mean?" Neil said. "We need a new one but we can't afford it."

"God damn it!" Anna kicked her way out and stood fuming in the driveway. "This promises to be some evening!"

When Jeff and Dolores got to the restaurant, they asked about the Papineau Room. They found that David, following Louise's orders, had booked it in the name of Dr. Wallis—his wife's degree title and born name—although he hated her usual pretense that she was a medical doctor. The waiters, who knew she wasn't, would joke about it. They would ask "Dr. Wallis" for advice on their imagined aches and pains.

Tonight was no different. "Can you prescribe me some viagra, Doctor?" the head waiter smirked. "It's not for me, of course. It's for my ex-wife's new husband."

Louise ignored the man's bad taste, but with a broad smile acknowledged his wit: "Maybe you should try before you buy. It doesn't work for the real limpies, you know."

Her pointed nod and wink in David's direction, and David's crushed look, were not lost on Dolores, who walked in at that very moment and promptly challenged her.

"That's just plain nasty, Louise. What's the matter with you?"

"Oh, it's David. He was supposed to pick up my green silk dress for tonight and he forgot, as usual."

"I didn't forget," pleaded David. "I had to go to customs to clear a shipment."

"More useless stock! We're going to have one hell of a big bankruptcy sale!"

Dolores fumed; Jeff stood back, aloof. Neil and

Anna arrived by taxi and soon everyone was seated, A waiter appeared and they ordered drinks and began looking at the menu.

"Happy birthday!" Dolores said, gritting her teeth and raising her glass to the sullen Anna. The others followed suit.

Making a huge effort, Anna responded, "Thank you all, this is lovely. And by the way, I really like your dress, Louise"; then, with a glance at Dolores, "...both your dresses."

"David forgot to pick up the green silk," Louise informed her. "Typical!"

She leaned over and gazed at Anna's near-schoolgirl garb. "But that's an interesting outfit you're wearing. It reminds me of when you were training as a nurse. The doctors used to kid you about being a convent-bred nymphomaniac."

"They were wrong about the convent," Dolores muttered.

"And about the nymphomaniac part," added Neil.

Anna glared at him. "What the hell does that mean? Anyway, you're no expert. And if you're not satisfied you can just leave."

"Oh, Neil's a connoisseur," David put in, grinning.

"What are you going on about?' Louise challenged him. He crumpled immediately.

"...just meant that Neil has a good appreciation of women."

"God, I'm sick of all you rabbity men," Anna muttered.

"I think Anna looks beautiful in that dress," Neil asserted, trying both to change the subject and regain the strong ground.

"Anna would look beautiful in anything," David put in.

"She'd look beautiful in nothing," said the usually tight-lipped Jeff.

Anna was suddenly blushing.

"Of course her outfit's pretty old," mumbled Neil, clearly aced in the compliment poker.

"Old—it's positively shabby," pronounced Louise, falling eagerly into the roll of dissenter. "But then Anna always does manage to dress like a bag lady."

A hush fell over the table.

Dolores was the first to recover. "That's outrageous, Louise—absolutely unacceptable."

The others chimed in, crying "Shame! shame!" in several ways and at various levels of intensity.

Unperturbed, Louise ordered more drinks and began to hum a little bit of *Traviata*. Her mother had lavished music lessons on her as a child, hoping to produce a new Peggy Lee or Joni Mitchell. Louise had become an amateur singer, but scorned pop music of all kinds and was busy these days studying famous operatic arias. Only a couple of years before she had known nothing about the subject, but now it was her reigning passion.

"You realize that I'm having a recital next month," she reminded them. "You're all invited, of course. I'll wear my green dress that evening, I promise you."

"If David doesn't forget to pick it up," Neil put in.

Dolores smiled and Anna glared at him.

"By that time it won't matter" said Louise, looking a trifle enigmatic.

"I think we should toast David for arranging this wonderful evening," Dolores said. Everyone paused, a little surprised...then they raised their glasses.

There sat David at one end of the table, pudgy, round-faced, and suddenly abashed at all this attention—his benign countenance masking an uneasiness that must surely derive from the need for a good smoke.

"It's wonderful to celebrate Anna's birthday," he ventured. "I wish we could do it every year."

"Oh, yes! Happy Birthday! Happy Birthday, Anna!" voices chimed in from around the table.

"Libiamo, libiamo," crooned the irrepressible Louise. She got up, danced a few steps, swayed from side to side, and sang, as if before a mirror, the words of the doomed Violetta:

Sempre libera degg'io
Folleggiar di gioia in gioia.

"Forever free, I must pass madly from joy to joy!" she translated. "Isn't it wonderful? I think we can all identify with that!"

Anna and Neil looked at each other, Jeff frowned, and Dolores closed her eyes. David reached for his glass to propose another toast and knocked it over.

The waiter came in, paused respectfully, then inquired with a smile, "Is the doctor's party ready to order now?"

Confirmation

The day she was scheduled to be confirmed in the Episcopal Church of America, Melanie took pictures of her son sleeping with his girl-friend.

She'd crept downstairs to make herself some herbal tea and caught sight of them, twined together on the farm's big living room sofa. At first she'd hesitated, about to close the door, then stood just inside the kitchen, feeling the sun already warm on her back, sipping her tea and regarding them with mingled guilt and pleasure.

Her son stirred on the couch; the girl moaned and reached a bare white arm toward him. Melanie smiled to herself, but was embarrassed. The covers had come down and one of the girl's breasts was visible. Simon looked dopey and beautiful, his long face pale as a spectre's. There was a faint smell of pot in the air. Melanie knew she ought to get out of there; ought to go and make noise in the kitchen, sing to herself, turn on the radio, make them get up. But she wanted to see more; she just couldn't pull herself away.

Had Bill ever held her like that? She couldn't be sure. She could hear him now, snoring and coughing fitfully in their room upstairs. He had a cold; he was tired. He'd been up all night reading some obscure book on Ezra Pound's poetry. He himself was writing a book of poetry, one that might never get published. But he ignored that, and only complained about how the farm work and his high school teaching threatened to swallow his energies. On the side he ran an organic flour milling operation, making just enough to cover expenses, sometimes a little more. He kept waiting for Simon to take an interest in the business; kept talking about someday getting a big contract—then he could retire as a schoolteacher, grind and sell his flour for profit, and write poetry. He clung to his vision of himself as a poet-farmer. She'd known for a long time that he would never be a successful businessman.

Melanie stepped quickly into the kitchen. An idea

had come to her, one that made her pulse jump with excitement. She found her Asahi Pentax hanging on a peg beside the pantry and, with trembling hands, lifted it down.

She'd bought the camera second-hand to help with her portrait- painting. Carlos, her art school teacher, had suggested it (rather than an "easy" digital one). Carlos, with his pot belly, his streaked white beard, and his clever hands spent much of the time trying to get her into bed. She'd never really been tempted, despite his whispered flattering conversations and his encouragement of her art, but she was too lethargic to get rid of him. Besides, he was a good teacher. Bill tolerated it, the way he tolerated everything. He wanted her to get "freed up," he said. He often told her that she was spiritless, depressed, uninterested in him. As if she didn't know; as if he understood anything about it.

She remembered how Bill had gone for a coffee while she lay down on her therapist's wide couch and let him touch and probe her body with his mechanical hands. The doctor's eyes bulged, he'd gotten more and more excited, until finally, wheezing and puffing, he'd entered her.

"How did it go?" Bill asked her later, driving back to the farm from the city. "Did it work the way he said it would?"

She hadn't thought she'd be embarrassed, but her cheeks had burned at the question. She couldn't look at her husband; she hated the leer in his voice, the inappropriate humour, the slight breathless hitch that betrayed the underside of his question.

After that, she'd fallen into months of deep depression. Heavy drugs and her painting classes had helped pull her out of it. Then she'd made the decision to join the Church. For a few days she'd felt transformed, almost radiant. But now, on the very day of her biggest commitment, her confirmation, she was uncertain.

She snapped the cover off the camera and tiptoed to the door of the living room.

She stood trembling, anxiously watching the young people, wondering if she dared to do it. Then took a step forward, looked at them through the viewfinder, held the camera away and waited. They moved and stirred again.

The girl, Amber, took a deep breath, and made a pleasant kind of whimpering noise. She sounded content. A sturdy local farm girl, a girl her son would surely drop when he went off to college. Yet Melanie envied her now, envied her round, strong face, her perfect rosy skin, her sleepy contentment and apparent fulfilment. How could she be so relaxed, so complacent, naked on someone else's couch? Melanie's father would have killed her if she'd done such a thing.

This was a kind of miracle, though, one for which she herself was partially responsible. She had never minded Simon bringing his girlfriends home, never objected to them sharing a room. He'd been doing it since he was sixteen. Now he was a strapping eighteen-year old, soon going off to college, and she hadn't the heart to change anything. She anticipated, with a kind of terror, the emptiness of the house when he left for good.

Ever since he was a little boy she had been open with him, not minding if he caught her and Bill getting dressed, half-naked, or even making love together, (though Bill was always angry about these intrusions). She insisted on this freedom, though, determined not to make the same mistake as her parents, who had lived for forty years in a state of seething hostility, and who—as her mother confided—never touched each other, never even undressed in each other's presence.

Melanie hadn't wanted that to happen to her. She hadn't wanted her son to grow up witnessing such a frozen and hopeless married life. And Simon had succumbed to her wishes; he seldom closed the door of his room; never attempted to hide himself when he came out of the shower. Melanie remembered the first time she had caught a glimpse of his mature body, the shock it gave her when she noticed the muscles, the sprouting dark hair between his legs, the changes. It made her realize how quickly her own life was passing.

She thought now she might take the first pictures without the flash. The flash might wake them up. She adjusted the lens and stepped across the room, barefoot on the soft broadloom, catching a glimpse of herself in the long mirror as she moved. Her own reflected image stopped her. She looked strained and guilty, she thought, thin and insubstantial in her white, flowing night gown.

Momentarily distracted, she shook her head, regretting her own appearance, the gray straight hair, her flushed rough cheeks and forehead. She was neither young nor beautiful. Yet inside her, and shining in her eyes, as she looked in the mirror, she sensed energy; a wild strength that sometimes overcame the darkness. In the past she had felt herself a powerful woman: giving birth to Simon; painting pictures—and sometimes, when she was alone, in her garden, or just walking in the fields, a sense of joy overcame her, of gratitude for being in the world. She had often wondered why she could give Bill nothing of that joy, why it always seemed to die in his presence.

She turned back to the sleepers, aimed the camera and began to snap her pictures.

The mechanism clicked much too loudly. Was she doing something foolish? It was Sunday and the church service was scheduled for eleven. Perhaps it wasn't right to do this on such a day?

Yet she couldn't stop.

Simon moved, rolled toward the back of the sofa and away from the girl, pulling the covers with him. Melanie could see her son's strong bare shoulders, the smooth curve of his back just above the rump. Amber, who must have felt his body shift, sighed, and leaned toward him, pressing her lips against his neck, still hardly awake, murmuring to herself. The girl's dark hair lay spread out against the white coverlet; she reached across Simon's hips— her whole upper body was bare now—and groped to touch him, perhaps to stroke him in the secret recesses under the blankets.

Melanie stepped closer and used the flash. She snapped picture after picture, circling the sofa. Soon she was wild with excitement, laughing to herself, in a kind of frenzy. She loved them, these two children, for they were children, after all, and not much more. She loved the sight of them together, their lazy unselfconscious sensuality, their youth and connection with each other.

Melanie circled the room; it opened to her, transformed and wonderful, illuminated by successive camera flashes, with the sunlight struggling to burst through the curtains. The icons, pictures, mementos, her treasures gathered on the walls and shelves, shone forth suddenly around her, leapt out from the decor: a Bar Mitzvah temple scene painted by her father, a photograph of Sai Baba, shrouded with a faded lotos blossom, and hung with a small yellowing package containing ashes materialized by that avatar; a few palm branches from a Sunday service; a picture of Jesus.

A long journey—her life-journey, with Bill reluctantly in tow—trying to escape the darkness, looking for happiness, for peace, for certainty, for God. And now in an instant, peering at the young people through the viewfinder, she saw their fresh bodies more and more awake, an awareness beginning to dawn in their startled, sleepy faces, Melanie felt herself shaken and moved, ecstatically present and happy.

It was a miracle. She knew everything, felt everything at once. Sensuality, nakedness—these were good. The sunlight, the shape of this room: wonderful. Being free and embracing the world; youth and pleasure and stripping away reserve— these were godlike and fulfilling, exactly what she had sought in her long quest through religions and cults, what she had always wanted for herself. She knew it now and realized that it had been always with her, a secret source, expressed in passing moments, when she stood in the kitchen, for example, scrubbing saucepans, mixing batter for bread—almost any time, sheer happiness threatened to overcome her—something she could never make Bill understand.

Joy, she thought, *joy*. The camera stopped working. The film had run out. Simon sat up, glaring at her and rubbing his eyes. Amber dived under the blankets.

"Sorry!" Melanie told them, but she wanted to hug them, counting on their forgiveness.

She retreated to the kitchen. She went the counter and put a disc in the machine: the B Minor Mass.

Underneath the rousing "Hosannas!" she heard heavy footsteps on the stairs, Simon's deep voice grunting and complaining in the next room.

Melanie stuck her head around the door. "Breakfast.... Should I make you some breakfast?" she called out. It was a plea for forgiveness, but Amber had disappeared into the bathroom. And Simon, blankets wrapped guiltily about him, stood regarding her with puzzlement, and what seemed like scorn.

"Taking pictures!" he said. "What did you do that for, mother?"

She shook her head. The joy was gone now. Bill was thumping down the stairs.

"I...don't know," she said truthfully, and turned away. She wanted to smash the camera, to throw it through one of the bright kitchen windows.

She stood over the sink, running water into the kettle. She heard Bill talking to Simon in the next room, but could not understand the words. The music blared: *Hosanna in Excelsis!*

Bill stuck his head through the kitchen doorway.

"Amber stayed the night," he said. "Did you know that Amber stayed the night?"

She nodded; she couldn't speak.

"What's the matter with you? I hope you're not depressed again today of all days! What time is the service?"

"Eleven o'clock."

She managed to get the words out. It seemed absurd to her now, going to church, making a commitment to God. She wanted to crawl upstairs and go to sleep forever in the dark empty bedroom.

"I asked Simon to stick around and help me—I've got to take the pickup over to Winchester," Bill went on. "They promised to work on it first thing Monday. Now he says he's going somewhere with Amber."

"I guess he forgot," she almost whispered. She knew Bill didn't really care when he took the truck in. It was Simon's obsession with Amber that was bothering him. The fact that they had made love under his roof.

"I'll drive over with you," she said. "After the service. We could stop and get my landscape sketch from Carlos."

There, she had said it, but she didn't care. It was the landscape sketch she wanted. Something of her own to work on.

"I don't want to see Carlos today. That's the last thing I want to do," he said.

He had come into the kitchen and stood there watching her. She turned, caught sight of his small compact figure, bristling and hostile now—and immediately turned away.

"He and Marsha said something about having

drinks. After the confirmation, I mean."

"Carlos? Why didn't you mention it? You know I have to take the truck in, to work on my book!"

He was furious, she knew, appealing to her, and yet there was nothing she could say. She had started to grind the coffee. The machine made a loud noise.

"Why were you taking pictures?" he shouted. "Why in hell were taking pictures of those two?"

"I'll explain, just leave me alone, will you? Leave me alone."

She couldn't look at him—didn't want him to see her face, her helpless tears. She couldn't bear another moment of his vicious pity.

Outside, the sunlight lay on her garden, on the fields beyond.

When he was gone, Melanie turned and caught sight of the camera where she had tossed it, a black lumpish thing in a basket full of tangled clothes and towels. For a moment she considered taking action: seizing the camera and exposing the film, ripping it out and shredding it to bits right there, strewing the kitchen floor with that sign of her repentance. Was that the act God demanded of her, that she should give up her impulses and her joy?

She began to cut some bread for toast. Then she stopped, turned, fetched the camera and dropped it quickly into a drawer, the extra deep bottom drawer in which she kept a few private things: her garden notebook, some of her figure sketches, and the nearly life-long records of her dreams.

A few minutes later, Bill came in and asked about breakfast.

"We should be leaving pretty soon," he reminded her.

He stood beside the laundry basket, a book in his hand, the sun flickering on his glasses. He seemed humbled, almost apologetic.

She started to speak, found the words hard to get out, and stopped.

She knew he was waiting for her to soften, to accept his chastened mood. "I'm not going," she said. "I've changed my mind. You can call Father Johnson."

He took a step toward her. His expression told her that he had expected this—another one of her perverse shifts of mind.

"For God's sake...." He shrugged his shoulders, swung his book back and forth, then tossed it carelessly into the laundry basket.

"I give up." He sat down at the kitchen table, continuing to look at her.

"It's all right, I'll get in touch with Father Johnson

myself. I'm going to see him right away. You can get the breakfast for everyone."

She stacked the pieces of cut bread on the counter and ran upstairs without looking at him.

When she came down, some minutes later, Bill was standing in the hallway by the front door. He had turned the music off.

"This is crazy," he said. "Changing your mind like this."

She didn't answer, but slipped past him, climbed into their sedan, hesitated a moment, then started the engine and pulled away slowly from the house.

In the sunlight her garden looked radiant and full, replete with spring vegetables, surrounded by her beloved early-blooming perennials—indigo plants and peonies and oxeye daisies. In its profligate richness, the garden made her think of Simon and Amy, of their young lives momentarily blooming in a mindless sensual tangle. She drove past the garden slowly, reluctantly, almost tempted to stop and walk the long stone path into the fields. But that was impossible, for Bill was certain to join her—Bill with his incomprehension and his questions—and she wouldn't have known how to talk to him, what words to use to convince him that he must accept her, once and for all, as she was, with all her strange moods and contradictions.

She couldn't wait for him, for how would she explain that he was simply wrong, that she hadn't changed her mind at all? That she had decided to go all by herself to her confirmation?

Intruders

Malcolm groaned and opened his eyes. His wife's heavy breathing sounded beside him. Staring up at the ceiling, anticipating what was coming, he waited with clenched hands for the signal.

After a few seconds he heard it. A loud rapping, as if someone was striking the walls or the kitchen table with a metal implement.

His body shook with disgust. He threw off the covers and slipped from the bed.

The floor was cold under his feet. He hesitated, staring down at Laura. A vague huddled shape, she lay unmoving, her breath a sustained sigh, like a murmur of broken dream-stuff.

There it was again. He shivered and took a step.

The floorboards creaked—if she woke she might think he was sleepwalking.

It didn't matter; he had to go down and face it.

He smiled bitterly, remembering another night, barely a year ago. He'd been up reading late and had found her at the head of these same narrow stairs, sleepwalking, calling out another man's name.

There it was again—he couldn't bear it.

He moved down the stairs, treading quietly, remembering the time after they had separated. When she agreed to return he'd worked long hours in order to restore the old farmhouse. How he'd struggled in the kitchen and on this narrow stairwell, determined to strip the paint and stain the wood, in order to give Laura a surprise. He remembered the whining machinery, the vibration of the sander, clouds of sawdust clogging his nose and throat. Later, he'd hired carpenters to renovate the kitchen and the old porch, increasing his already heavy debt to do it.

When Laura came back from the west after their separation, she seemed surprised and happy at the changes, and even offered to take another job to help pay the bills. But he didn't want her travelling the forty-five miles to the city. Too much had gone wrong when she did that. Now they were thinking of having a baby, scraping by on what he could make as a freelance writer with very few publishing connections.

Silence—but the stairs creaked as he reached the bottom. He heard a scurrying nearby and hesitated. Then took a deep breath, reached over, and switched the light on.

Everything seemed in order, everything looked bright, clean and pleasant—the round oak table, the old cook stove, the new fridge and the not-so-new electric stove, the open shelves lined with crockery and bottles

He walked around the table, then groaned as he stooped to pick up a large potato from a place near the door. Partially eaten, it had been pushed or carried from a small open bin beside the electric stove. He saw turds on the rim of the bin. The rats had broken in. Somehow they'd got in again, despite the refurbishing, the metal lining above the baseboards, the new plaster.

"Malcolm," his wife called from upstairs. *"Are you all right, Malcolm?"*

He swore under his breath: at least she'd got his name right this time. Stepping warily across the cold floor, he opened the kitchen door and pitched the potato into the darkness of the yard. He closed the door; as he did so he caught a glimpse of their sheepdog, Sasha, stretching his paws and yawning from his bed on the porch.

"I'm all right, but they're back," he shouted up to her. "The goddamned things are back."

The kitchen seemed suddenly polluted. All that work, that money put out for nothing. And the noise: why did they have to make so much noise?

He went over to the cupboards, warily opened a door, and took out a bottle of Jameson. Fetching a glass, he poured himself a drink.

"Why don't you come back to bed?" his wife called.

It might have been an invitation, although her voice sounded bored. Since their reunion, their love-making had become desperate, and even passionate, but with very little closeness. He had begged her, out of curiosity, and because it aroused him, to tell him about her affair, but she had indignantly refused. She wouldn't even let him read her precious diaries or letters—and threatened to leave him if he pried too much. They were together now and that was all that mattered, she insisted.

That might be true, but it didn't help. He found himself obsessed with what she had experienced with the other man. Since she would tell him nothing, he had to rely on his own imagination and it had trapped him well and good. Lurid thoughts came at him unexpectedly, unwanted; and yet he enjoyed them, wallowed in them. Like a drug habit innocently acquired, his fantasies proved destructive to his peace of mind, yet they were endlessly compelling. And sometimes, when he held his wife close, anger took hold of him. Her sighs of pleasure, he thought, must be play-acting. She seemed like a stranger to him. He wasn't even sure he wanted a child with her.

The next morning, they cleaned the kitchen together. They removed the potatoes from the bin and threw most of them out.

"They must be getting in from the shed," Laura said. She grilled some bacon and made toast in the oven. They sat at the round table with their coffee. She looked pretty in her white bathrobe, untidy, yawning a little and smiling at his restlessness.

"Too bad about the noise," she said. "I must have been tired, though. I went right back to sleep."

"I'm going to check everything," he told her.

Using a flashlight he searched the corners of the kitchen, seeking a hole, an entry point. He moved the fridge and cupboards a little, scowling at the dusty floor. On his hands and knees he examined the wall behind the cook stove, where it joined the outside shed. Everything was sealed tight. He stood considering. The kitchen looked wonderful, alive with pleasant sounds: the hissing of the kettle, the warm crackle of the morning fire, the sizzling of the bacon in the pan.

"I'll go get a trap," he said.

His wife looked at him. "Maybe it's a good idea...I want to do some washing—mind if I don't go?"

He drove to the nearby village, past the scrub farms with their ramshackle houses. Tall silos stood up in the sunshine, the sturdy barns already packed with hay. It was Saturday, and not many people were at work. Everyone would be heading for the shopping centres or visiting the local flea-market, selling to each other the old dishes, the furniture and tools of their grandparents, or dealing them off, at inflated prices, to strangers from the city.

He suddenly felt the sadness of these country people, the gloom that seethed beneath their heartiness. They bragged constantly about their friendliness, chatted to him about the weather and other trivia, but otherwise treated him warily, almost with suspicion. To them he was an outsider.

Two years before, he and Laura had escaped from their town apartment, looking for space and freedom, but after a while they had found that the old farmhouse was making them poor. So many repairs were needed that she had little to spend, and her friends seldom came to visit. They argued about money, passing too much time together. After she got the job in the city, after her affair, Malcolm wondered if they had made a terrible mistake, if they had ruined their chances together by moving to the country.

At the hardware store in the village he picked up the rat traps, some Wayfarin, and fresh batteries for his flashlight, joking with Garth, the owner— somewhat uneasily—about "the varmints." He drove home slowly, wondering who would buy the house if they decided to sell it, and whether he could get work in the city.

"Those traps look awful," Laura said, as he tumbled them out on the kitchen table. "Do they have to be that big?"

"I won't use the poison unless I have to," he promised. "We don't want Sasha getting sick."

That night he took some raw hamburger for bait, and set the trap on the floor between the stove and fridge.

He and Laura shared a bottle of wine and made love in bed later. He slept right through to morning, but when the brilliant sunshine woke him, he lay for a while, wondering if his memory of a noise in the night had been just a dream.

He crept downstairs. No sign of disturbance in the kitchen. It was puzzling. But when he wandered into the adjoining room to start a fire, he saw it.

It lay beside the wood stove in the living room, still alive, a rat squirming under the metal bar and staring up at him with eyes full of terror and pain.

The creature looked healthy and vicious, almost fat, but its back was clearly broken and the brutal trap mechanism still held it. It must have crawled here from the kitchen, dragging its rubbery white tail behind it. Sickened, Malcolm grabbed the poker and struck at it. It was like hitting a piece of meat. The rat died without a sound.

He found a garbage bag, tore at it with trembling hands and dropped the bloodied thing and the trap into its green plastic depths.

"What are you doing down there?" Laura called.

He stood by the kitchen table, shivering, taking deep breaths to calm himself. *"We got the bastard!"* he called up to her....

During the next few months they passed many peaceful nights. He felt as if he had recovered the house for them. Yet their problems continued. The car broke down; water got in through the chimney.

More repairs and more debt. Then winter came on suddenly and every day he faced the harsh weather. The driveway piled up with snow, and the farmer who plowed it was always late.

Laura sank into a kind of lethargy. They argued constantly; she was lonely, she said: she had to get out of the house. She began making trips to the city.

One day when he came down for breakfast he found that the electric stove wouldn't work. He checked the plug and fuses, the circuit breaker in the basement, but it was no good. He could have cried out in despair—they would have to get a new stove, and where was the money to come from? Laura said she would have to go back to work. She needed a change; she was fed up, sitting around all day in the middle of nowhere.

He drove to the village and picked out a second-hand stove at the electrical shop. The man assured him it would work; he'd even give them a six-month guarantee. He said he'd bring the stove that afternoon and take away the old one.

When Malcolm returned he found Laura dressed up and waiting.

"I need to get out," she said. "I called Maggie and we're going to meet at the shopping centre. Don't worry, I won't spend very much...I just need a break, that's all."

Then, as if reading something else in his silence or his look, she added: "If you're worried about me, why not come too? You can do your own thing, can't you, while Maggie and I hang out together? I'd like your company on the way home."

"I don't want to go anywhere," he said. He felt ashamed of his own suspicions, of his sullenness. "I'll wait for the stove.... Maybe I'll make dinner for us."

When she drove away, the snowy outside world closed in. The brightness of the day seemed empty; the house creaked around him. It sounded like an old ship.

He sat down at the kitchen table, staring around the pleasant room. He got up and went to the fridge, but the beer had run out. He had work to finish but he couldn't write. He found himself depressed, close to tears.

He sat there and after a while the salesman came with the stove—a thin gnarled man with big hands and a pockmarked face. He looked around the kitchen with interest.

"Been doing some work in here, I see. Never looked like this when Dick Casselman had it."

Together they started to wrestle the old stove out

of its niche in the corner. They bumped it from side to side, not working well together. Malcolm noticed with disgust that the metal sides were caked with grime. Hadn't he and Laura cleaned it just a few months ago? The floor beneath was again thick with dust. Where did it all come from?

"Ain't in very good shape," the man said, peering into the oven. "Don't think I'll want to take this one. I'll have a look, though."

With a screwdriver he attacked the back of the stove. The metal plate, held by only two screws, came away easily.

Malcolm sat at the kitchen table, fingering the knobs of the replacement stove, watching him. He was feeling intruded upon, ashamed of everything: of his house, of the renovations that had once made him proud, of his debts—of the helplessness of his life.

Then the man stood up suddenly. He stared across at Malcolm but said nothing.

"What is it?"

"See here," the man said, pointing.

Malcolm squeezed in behind the stove. He peered inside. Beside a nest of frayed wires, pressed flat against a metal plate, he saw three dark shapes, bloodless and desiccated: baby rats, starved to death, with skin you could peel away if you cared to touch them.

"Had some visitors?" the man said.

Malcolm closed his eyes. He remembered the unquiet darkness, the violence in his hands when he raised the poker.

They had not broken into the house. After the carpenters had done their work they had been trapped there, all of them, the mother he had killed and the baby rats.

When the appliance man had driven away, Malcolm locked out the dog and sat unmoving in the kitchen. The thought of the rats disturbed him; he couldn't get them out of his mind. He listened, but heard only the muffled whimpering and the scratching of their sheepodog on the porch, the drone of a car on a distant highway.

After a while, he glanced at his watch. It was late. Why hadn't Laura come back from the city?

He recalled his vague promise to make dinner, but now he had no appetite. He felt drugged, his arms and legs heavy. Frightened by the deadness inside him, he pressed his hands against his chest, as if trying to locate his own beating heart.

For some minutes he sat numbed, then he remembered Laura's letters and diaries, the ones she'd stashed in an old suitcase at the back of the closet in their bedroom. She had forbidden him to read them, but now the compulsion came and he could not resist it. He felt helpless beside her, ignorant of what she really felt and thought. If he could only find something, a secret diary, a description of what she had experienced with the other man, if only he could gaze at her photographs, read her love letters, or discover some half-obscene exchange that would be strong enough, shocking enough, to give substance to his constant fear and pain.

Frantic, he sprang up, taking the narrow stairs two at a time. In the bedroom, he stopped. His own fierce breathing filled the room. But he sensed Laura's presence there too, and it daunted him. To go any further might be to risk everything.

He groaned softly—a kind of release—threw open the cupboard doors, pulled her clothes out, and tossed them on the floor. As he grabbed at her favourite blue dress, it snared on a hanger. He twisted out the wire and flung it against the dresser mirror. He tore at the dress and threw it aside. He pushed away a trunk and hauled out Laura's old tan suitcase. He slammed it on the bed, fumbled with the latches and got it open.

He began to rifle through her papers. Tossing away the familiar postcards and some high school photographs, he found an envelope that some groping instinct told him was different from the rest.

He ripped it open, spilling the contents on the bed. Frantically, he turned over each paper in turn. He could not believe his eyes. It was merely a set of clippings about places they had visited, foreign sights they had once enjoyed. He felt deceived, put upon.

His failure to find anything incriminating alarmed him. He went through everything in the suitcase. It contained some printed manuscript pages, stories she must have written and stashed away. He read them anxiously, but could make nothing of them. They seemed rarefied, poetic, innocuous. Her diaries were full of nature poems and quaint drawings. There were old birthday cards, bits of fragile lace, letters from her grandmother, and photographs of her childhood pets—a Corgi, a canary, a Siamese cat.

Her feminine sweetness, her essential goodness struck him with the force of an unspoken accusation. The room took shape around her absent spirit, pressing on him with the gravity of a simple truth.

He lay down on the bed, cradled there by his wife's

clothes, the diary pages, the lace, and the birthday cards, addressed to her and inscribed "with love" by him.

After a while he heard the barking of a dog. For a moment he imagined that the Corgi in the photograph had greeted him. But of course it was only Sasha, their lively sheepdog, tied up outside and impatient for his early evening walk. Malcolm ignored the summons, pressing his palms against his shut eyes, alert for some other signal. He lay there a long time, waiting for the sound of their car, fearful of what was coming in his life.

Storm Warnings

That day it was stormy, a blur of cold light, fierce wind, and snow blowing everywhere. Mila went to the window and stared out. A wild March, and Easter not far away.

She groaned aloud, shivered, crossed the kitchen and dropped one of the last pieces of cut wood into the ancient cook-stove, then closed the cover plate and went back to her work on the molding.

She'd stripped the old paint from the top of the door frame nearly to the floor, and the bare wood shone with a deep honey luster. She'd rubbed in the warmed-up linseed oil, and although the exposed wood was still nearly as pitted and gashed as a mottled, time-worn cliff, it gave her a certain pleasure.

In fact her whole farmhouse, shabby and beautiful, almost gave her pleasure. Even on days like this, when she was alone, and almost forced to stay indoors, the sight of the place could almost cheer her.

Her work on their house, she knew, was also a kind of therapy, for it served to keep her stray, dangerous thoughts at bay. John, her husband, was right, she was a dreamer, and the contents of her dreams seemed to have no limits. Had several of her day-dreams been described to him as another woman's, he would have called them salacious, or maybe even disgusting; had he known they were hers, it would have given him the shock of his life.

She shook her head, sat down at the kitchen table and sipped at her lukewarm tea. Through one window she could see the chill, stark world that their fields had become. The blizzard that had begun the night before had already half-obliterated some familiar landmarks—the huge old barn with its rusted roof, the sheds, a stand of maples near an array of junked cars that were a perpetual eyesore from almost every angle. Those cars—rusted, ugly, useless even as scrap—how she wished they might be buried forever by the snow, or picked up by some freak wind and cast away into the middle of the scrub wood that lay beyond their back acres.

John had promised to get rid of those cars long ago, and had innocently hired some conniving local to do the job, but the man had gone off with their money and left the cars.

Other memories, bigger failures, came to mind. Oh yes, their romance had been full of the cruel poetry that scars you forever and makes it impossible to let go of the affections and memories that are born there. Seven years of arguments and recriminations, seven years of going nowhere and producing nothing, seven years of watching her man being almost—but never quite—drawn away by the charms of other women couldn't quite break her attachment.

Though John's behaviour had seemed to threaten her, it was she who had crossed the forbidden boundaries. She'd assumed, almost unconsciously, that when she'd violated their marriage pact, or had it breached for her, she could escape from her lingering ties to her husband. But it hadn't worked out like that. Her lovers, first Ron, and now Mark (John, self-centered, oblivious, knew nothing of either) were vulnerable and human, and had their own absurd demands, but she still felt unable to go further, mired in her marriage and her isolation, saved from depression only by her daily handicrafts and housework, her reading, and her dreams.

Right now, for example, her thoughts took a strange turn: she began to imagine a visit from one of her "secret men.". Such a thing was against all odds in this fearsome storm, yet the fantasy was so vivid that she thought she heard a car in the driveway. A voice, a man's attention, even a telephone call just then would have soothed her, and although she was far from ready to initiate any contact, she would have rejoiced had it happened

Uneasy, she stepped across the kitchen, remembering that she had some tidying to do in the front room parlour. At the same time she was thinking: *where has that dog got to?* Sadko, their Husky, had disappeared that morning shortly after John drove off to work. Perhaps he'd crawled into the barn for shelter. Or possibly, in the manner of his breed, he was revelling in the snow, half-buried and happy in some nearby drift. Maybe she would wander out later and try to find him. Maybe it was a good reason to get some air, to face the bad weather and even enjoy it, to help disperse her wayward thoughts.

She slipped across the kitchen, heading toward

the parlour cupboard, but stopped at the doorway and glanced around. The kitchen's wood frames and moldings, the rough birch floor, the battered pots hanging up on the wall—they gave her pleasure. The ancient cook-stove, the heavy cast-iron chandelier and the narrow stairway leading mysteriously upstairs—so many things about the room suited her. Even the creaking and groaning of the old house-beams under the pressure of the storm winds wasn't threatening

John had given her one of his "little jobs" before he left for the university. He seemed to think that if he didn't suggest something she would drift through the whole day in a waking dream. There was some truth in that, yet it was also proof of how little he knew her. He would be shocked, horrified, if he'd discovered how she'd spent some of her housebound days only weeks before. He took her moods and whims for granted, and expected her to surprise him, as he'd told her, with demands and complaints that he couldn't deal with. He knew that she could be very moody, depressed and violently resistant. But his icy critiques never reached down to the possibility of her betrayal; he hadn't even come close to the possibility that in turning away from their intimacy she might embrace someone else. Which was exactly what had happened, and more than once.

How typical of John, the busy professor and incompetent husband, the distracted, crude optimist, the sharp-tongued guy she was stuck with because she remembered him as a wonderful life-saving lover, full of energy and promise.

She walked through their main sitting room, a big space, but elegant with its white wallpaper, tin ceiling, and ancient woodstove. The large windows gave more views of the fields, of the swirling snow, and the paved back road that led to town, half-hidden by the storm, looked even more desolate than usual.

That morning John had struggled to get their car down their unpaved driveway and out to that road. She'd had to go out and push, and he'd finally got traction and skidded along, the old oversized sedan creeping away and finally disappearing into the snow-swept distances. He was due back at five o'clock, around sunset.

She stepped into the front room, an old-fashioned parlour they hardly ever used, and pulled open the cupboard built in under the main staircase.

Mila took a deep breath: the cupboard smelled of mothballs, scented candles, and pot. It was packed full of things, an odd assortment: old lamps, dishes, LP records, some broken toys, bags of gloves and socks. It made her sad to see the stuff, the detritus of their seven years together—John's notes and papers, bundles of magazines, some Christmas decorations, her teen diaries and school essays, cards and letters from friends and relatives.

At one point, in a rare fit of tidiness, they'd tossed all the family photos they possessed into a single large box, and John thought it was time to sort and separate them. Some of the photos were very old and had started to decay and to stick together: "the only time the Kristofs and the McVeighs will ever be that close," as he'd put it.

That was certainly true, Mila thought, as she searched for the right box. Her family, originally from France and Slovakia, had been farm people for generations; the McVeighs were urban Irish from Boston. Well aware that the two groups had nothing in common, John—with her tacit approval—had made sure that they met and mingled as seldom as possible. Even so, there had been a few quite comical and disastrous get-togethers. Now that John had decided to save the decaying photographs, he thought they should create two separate albums, one for each family. Did that indicate, she wondered, that he was newly obsessed with separations and splits, or was she, as usual, missing something obvious?

She spotted the box she thought might hold the photos at the back of the top shelf, an old hatbox, and quickly pushed a few LPs aside. She reached up and tried to pull it forward.

It didn't budge (why was the box so heavily?) She swore and kicked at one of the leather suitcases stacked just inside the door. The whole pile of suitcases began to topple. She reached over to steady it. Her fingers touched something glossy, a large card, slightly frayed. She fetched it down to examine it, and something clicked in her memory.

It was a greeting card, a bit oversized and ridiculous, and she turned it round in her fingers, gasping a little as recognition came.

It was the last card she'd ever received from her father.

She opened it and read the big scrawl of his writing: REMEMBER ME, was all it said, and John, her father, had signed it.

(Was it significant that she had fallen in love with and married an older man who had the same name as her father? It was a question her therapist had taken up with her more than once. But now angrily, she pushed the association from her mind as if it were a profanation of this moment, of this accidental but seemingly significant connection with her father's death).

She stepped back into the parlour, holding the card out, and turning it over and over in her slender white hands, surprised when a few of her tears dropped on it.

It was an Easter card written just about two years ago, barely a week before her father's death, a garish card with oversized lilies and scrolled gold-stamped lettering, and, though she had obviously supressed all memory of it, it struck her now with the force of a sign, or a portent.

She had forgotten that the second anniversary of his death was so close. He had died finally of a rare blood disease, which (as Maria, his girl-friend, had insisted) had probably come about a result of his old war wounds. Maria had persuaded her father to move with her to the suburbs after her mother's death five years before—she and John Kristof had been childhood sweethearts. Mila disliked her, and had treated her coldly, but she had to give the woman credit for standing by her father during his final illness.

The telephone call telling of her father's death

had come from Maria. Mila had been alone on the farm, or so she thought, when the news arrived; and she blamed her own John for not being there. It was irrational, she knew, but her anger at him was immense, overwhelming. She broke down completely, weeping and wandering outside. It was a warm day at the beginning of April and she drifted aimlessly up the driveway, until she found herself, somewhat dazed, beside the big barn. (If she had noticed that Ron Borton's pickup was parked nearby it was merely a subliminal perception.)

She swung the barn's battered wooden door back, latched it again and wandered in among the cattle stanchions. Her father had been a farmer for most of his life and somehow the barn spaces and smells, for once, seemed immediately consoling. The last time he had visited her she had showed him around the whole building, and listened to his shrewd comments and reminiscences about the past.

As she stood in the barn, the memory brought with it a new wave of sadness. His image flashed clearly in her mind, then a figure appeared from the shadows and she found herself face to face with Ron Borton.

Before they exchanged a word she knew that they would connect. It would happen inevitably, quickly.

He would take the lead and she would follow. The consequences didn't matter.

Borton had rented the farm-use from her husband shortly after they bought the place. He had leapt at the chance to take it on; anything to be able to hang around there, to be close to her. From their first meeting Mila was aware of how attracted he was to her; she was used to male attention, and could measure it precisely. John of course was oblivious. He had even posted a naked photograph of her in his farmhouse office. One male guest who had seen it had immediately vowed, quite seriously, to divorce his wife.

John had tried to be chummy with Borton and had even invited him and his oversized, jolly country wife to dinner. Borton himself was a short, stocky, muscular man with sharp flashing eyes, a ready smile and a witty tongue. John hadn't noticed how many of Borton's incidental remarks slyly mocked him. There were references to the "honey-dipper" they used at table; sarcastic comments about old men and their "antiques." (Borton was younger than John, about Mila's age). Later, when the affair began, John one day found Borton's underwear in their washing, but Mila had dismissed this with some roundabout implausible story.

She was astounded at her husband's blindness, but for some months quite grateful for it. Later, it occurred to her that it was a sign of his indifference to her and a signal that his attention was elsewhere. Still later she'd decided that was wrong; he was just plain naïve.

Staring at her father's Easter card she was overcome with memories not of John Kristof, but of her affair with Borton. She had felt safe in his arms, consoled and comforted. She didn't mind sleeping with him in the bed she and John had bought after their marriage, an old pine bed of character and strength. The bed was large and solid and while John was at work she shared it with her lover. Borton's strong body pleased her; he was passionate and in the end he was ready to take her away from "that antique fussy math prof" she was stuck with.

At that point Mila began to disengage from him. When she was younger she'd had a steady boyfriend, but she had occasionally slept with other young men. When she was twenty-two and his student, she and John had begun an affair that became the scandal of his department. When he left his wife and children for her, much to the astonishment of everyone, it seemed the perfect love-match. But she couldn't respond to his superior ways, she baulked at his tutelage, and he began to seem to want other women, though he'd hadn't bedded any, of that she was certain. Now, though she felt justified in her betrayal of John, she wasn't ready to cast him off for a man like Ron Borton, whose attractions were so fleeting and limited.

In fact when Borton found her pulling back a little he got desperate and foolish and began to brag about his bank account (saved from years of factory work and casual farming) and to promise her outlandish things.

But something else too made her draw back from Borton. When their affair really got going, and his visits to her bed and their grapplings in the barn become almost blatant, his contempt for her husband seemed to increase. She thought later that such an attitude must be typical of men who get into bed with other men's wives; at the time, however, she was too involved to think straight about such male problems or to worry about her marriage.

Borton, however, seemed suddenly to grow chummy with John and almost to become a buddy, apparently eager to help the oblivious math professor understand the mysterious ways of the country. Innocent enough, yet one day her lover urged her husband to use the tractor to pull out an annoying pole that the previous owners had planted near the front porch of the house. It was indeed an eyesore, but hard to remove. Borton kindly explained how John could hook up a chain to the tractor and drag it out. What he failed to explain that the chain had to be an appropriate length. When John drove the tractor forward the pole came tearing from the ground and slammed down hard on the tractor fender. It missed his head by a few inches and left a dent in the metal fender.

John was unhurt but taken aback. He lost interest in further lessons in farm work. Mila began to ease out of her relationship with Borton.

At John's urging she took a six-month contract job in the city. Although she commuted and slept at home it was a relief to escape the country and both of her men, even for a few hours a day. The industrial design company where she worked was staffed mostly by boring executives and preoccupied married men, but in the art department, which she had to visit daily as part of her routines, she met someone she had run into before, casually, at a few parties. He was, a young Chinese man named Mark Chow, the former boyfriend of a woman she did not like and who hated her. She and Chow had been mutually attracted from the first and things happened fast. Mila was very shapely and summer clothes favoured her, and the same was true of him. They spent lunch picnicking at a nearby park, gazing at each other, and ushering in the inevitable touch and feel. Finally, he took her to a motel where they drank champagne and made use of the condoms he had bought along the way. She was thrilled by his beauty; he was not very tall, but darkly handsome, slender and strong, a karate black belt. Many meetings followed; she would cut work and spend the day in his apartment. They made love, then she would put on the white terry cloth robe he'd bought her to match his, although she enjoyed watching him move naked around the room. Sometimes she just smoked pot and stroked him while he pretended to sleep. Their affair went on for months.

She told John about Mark, all except the important part, and once again she was astounded at her husband's blindness. One night she woke up, climbed out of their bed and started to sleepwalk toward the front of the house, calling out "Mark!" "Mark!" as she walked. John was in his office, working out some complex equations, and he intercepted her and settled her back in bed. She explained that she was just having a minor problem at the office.

Like Ron Borton, Mark invited her to go away with him, but John had a violent temper and she didn't want to risk it. She recognized that although she was infatuated with Mark, she wasn't sure she wanted to live with him.

Now summer and fall had passed and winter too had cycled round. Her office time was over, and although Mark had managed a couple of sneak visits to the country to sleep with her in her own bed, their meetings were becoming increasingly difficult. Besides, Ron—still living in hope—showed up from time to time and tried to bed her.

Now Easter was coming round again and here she stood with a message from her father in her hand. He had asked in his Easter card to be remembered, but it was her lovers she was remembering. Daydreaming, reviewing her past, she wondered what her life would become. Deep conviction told her that if she and John were to go on and make something of their marriage, she would have to confess her infidelities to him. Although she feared his reaction, and an outbreak of violence—a few had occurred already—she knew that her grip on him was strong. She knew that several very attractive women had tried to draw him away, but she was quite sure of him. She was the roving lover, not he, and that was her strength—and her weakness.

Clasping her father's card in one hand she returned to the kitchen. The afternoon was slipping away and the snow still falling. It was possible that John would leave early, before dark, but she should call him, talk to him and remind him to take special care in the storm.

She placed her father's card on the counter, stared at it for a moment, then thought: *why did I come on the card today of all days?* I should take it as a kind of notice or reminder, not to forget the past. *Remember me,* her father had told her—was telling her, perhaps from another reality—but she hadn't attended his dying, and had seldom thought of him afterward. This was her punishment: to be trapped here alone, thinking of her marriage, her husband, her lovers, but without much clarity, unable to decide on anything, or anyone.

But it wasn't too late. She lifted the card from the counter and crooned softly to herself: *O mio babbino caro,* O Daddy, I haven't decided what to do—I'm not like the girl in the opera, although I was once. I was sure of my love and my future, but I never really asked for your approval and help. I knew you disapproved of John—taking on a married man, an older man with two kids already—not a smart move, you made that clear. *But, Daddy, I did love him and we did have wonderful passion, and my life did seem to have some meaning for a while.*

She turned, wondering if her father, in some distant realm, could take this in. She closed her eyes and tried to evoke him: his slim strong body, always in motion, his knobby fingers, his white hair always rough-cut, his dark eyebrows quizzically raised; his hooked nose a little red from the drink.

No wonder he doubted and suspected her own John; her father wasn't remotely like her tall, slender, over-particular husband. Her father would have hit it off with Ronnie, though—a couple of rural smart guys, witty, earthy, and energetic, however limited in academic skills.

She closed her eyes and sent a thought to nowhere: *but, Daddy, if you think I made a mistake you're quite wrong…it's John that I was meant for.*

She remembered their romance, their shameless escapades and brazen connections, those awful weeks and months that preceded his final break from his first family. He was handsome and rather dashing in his way, and he had obviously adored her. They had settled in England, the two of them, and lived in a wonderful and terrible isolation and intensity. They cooked, made love, walked, read, and listened to music. She loved to listen to his thoughts on math, Mozart, or history.

Pure romance, and then marriage, all in isolation, and all magical, except that he was the leader, he set the tone, he had the power. His tyranny was sometimes harsh, and occasionally comical. Once, when they were living in an old house in Jesmond Dene, in Newcastle, enjoying an attic room in the huge place they'd rented from one of John's university colleagues, she managed to trump him. John had dragged himself out of their bed to work on a math problem; she stayed under the covers, cozy and naked as usual. As she lay there someone began playing the piano in the adjoining house. The sounds floated in through the wall, sustained and beautiful

"What's that incredible music?" she asked John, who knew his classics. This one, however, he couldn't identify. He mumbled something about "maybe Schumann" and told her it didn't matter. It was just one of the little girls next door practicing— quite ordinary. "No it's not!" she said. "It's someone very special."

Later that day they learned that the great Sviatoslav Richter had been next door practicing for a concert.

She had gone on to score other hits, to puncture more of John's over-inflated and oh-so-superior assumptions. She was quite hard on him and at first he didn't thank her for it, but in the end he seemed to enjoy her intuitions and brusque corrections. She wondered if it might be part of his masochism.

They had started out so unequal, except for her beauty. She knew that John was pleased that she had other gifts, but when she began to confound him with them, and impress other men, he grew sullen, resistant. He stood up to her more often and their exchanges became harsh and unyielding.

Her shrink had told her that her affairs were quite healthy; they showed that she was defining herself, he said, that she was becoming independent, taking her own path. Remembering her dependencies on her lovers, though, she had begun to think her doctor had overrated her. She didn't tell him that one day when they were driving out and John had insisted he was going to leave her, she had thrown herself from their moving car.

Now she talked to the card on the counter. "Look at me, Daddy, I'm a wreck," she said aloud. "I'm worried about John driving back, and yet I'm tired of being alone and would be happy if Mark dropped in suddenly. I just can't seem to walk a straight line."

She gazed at the Easter card for a long minute and then added: "I know what you think I should do. You think I should call John, make dinner for him, and try being a good faithful wife for a while."

She burst out laughing, choked a little, poured herself a glass of white wine then started the process of making John's favourite veal stew. When she had got it going, and assembled the meat, potatoes and carrots in the Creuset, she reached for the phone and dialed her husband's office number.

The phone rang at the other end; she was sure she'd get his voicemail, and wasn't surprised when his laconic message came on: *"Sorry, I'm not available...."* The voice droned on. "That's the problem," she said aloud, "you're never available when I need you."

She waited for the signal and started to talk. Her voice sounded nervous and hesitant, which annoyed her.

"I assume you're coming around five," she told him "Please be careful. It's been a weird day here, but I'm making dinner.... If the roads are too bad, maybe you should stay in town"

Now why had she said that? If he stayed in town

she'd be furious. She couldn't bear to spend the night alone. She'd have to call Mark, or anyone. Even one of her girlfriends....

She slammed the phone down, and in a burst of nervous energy, crossed the kitchen floor and climbed the stairs. These led directly into their small barely furnished bedroom; she flopped down on the pine bed, pulling the old-fashioned Hudson's Bay blanket over her legs and thighs. Images of clutching and cuddling and guilty love distracted her: why didn't she remember the thousands of times she'd slept here with John? What she remembered was Mark, his naked body stretched across the bed, the two of them making love like innocent children, or Ronnie's restless, muscular, roughly protective embrace. The contact with John she remembered most was the time during their first year together when they had both been laid low by flu and had spent days lying nearly inert in the big bed, dazed, half-comatose, dreaming, embracing, falling in and out of sleep. Was John her limbo lover, someone she could only enjoy in a strange half-life zone that lay beyond the real, the energized world?

She swore and rolled out of the bed, brushing at her jeans as if they had touched something contaminated. She stepped into the adjoining dressing room. It looked out over the back of the farm, over a few rundown sheds, a long twisting, half-fallen fence, over fields desolately beautiful now in the drifting snow. She pressed her hands against the streaked and smeared window panes and thought how in summer legions of houseflies seemed to rise from nowhere and swarm there. The Beelzebub window, John had called it, as he attacked the invaders with a spray can of lethal chemicals.

Mila felt sad, and thought she might burst into tears. But as she brushed at her eyes with the backs of her hands, something caught her attention, a noise from below. She listened, anxiously attentive to the sound, its quiet insistence, something moving in the kitchen; or scratching, clawing at the wood, trying to get in.

"Oh, God!" she said aloud. "Not a rat!"

She and John had fought the rats for a few years; the battle seemed hopeless. The creatures inhabited the sheds and barns and once or twice had roamed between floors in the house. Endless repairs to the woodwork, metal panels, dishes full of poison, kept them at bay. Yet their incursions seemed relentless. When they caught one, neither she nor John felt up to disposing of the trap. A neighbouring farm boy took care of that for them—for a price, and with a curious glee. It was a nightmare.

Now she had to face it. She had to go downstairs; the stew might be burning; the woodstoves would need fueling. If she banged a pot on the stove or shouted it might go away. She took a deep breath and slowly descended.

The kitchen looked tranquil; no huddled gray blots in the corners. Through the windows she could see the yard and the barns; everything so clean in the gusts of snowy wind.

She stood at the kitchen table, listening and watching. At first she heard nothing, then, from the other side of the outside doors, the scratching sounds, accompanied now by a high-pitched desperate whining. She smiled, relieved, because she recognized the sound. She crossed to the door and pushed up the latch. With an effort, she shoved the inside door back. Through the glass of the outer door the yard's swirling snow resembled a scene from a maniac's snow-globe. Looking down through the door panel she caught a glimpse of the gray twisted form of an animal. It crouched there, its head turned away, half-buried in a drift.

It was Sadko, their Husky, wanting in at last.

She leaned her whole weight against the glass

door, attempting to move it. As it opened she could hear their dog's whimper of pain. She pushed harder, frustrated by her lack of strength.

The wind blew, soiling the floor with a melting scurf of snow. The cold chilled her ankles, and she let the door go. It slammed shut.

She crossed the room and fetched one of the pokers on the cook-stove. The hot metal scorched her hand, and she dropped it. It clattered to the floor, making a slight hiss as it skipped across the streaks of snow.

She swore and reached for the door, pulling her sweater around her as she leaned her weight on it. She tried not to panic but her eyes were full of tears and her hand pained her. She got down on her hands and knees, and reaching around the door, began to dig with the poker, to scoop away the snow with her bare hands. Then she touched something sharp and pulled back, thinking she might have been bitten.

She went on digging, the wind in her face, until the door moved. She stood back, shivering and crying, to let the crouching gray shape tumble into the room.

When it looked up at her, she put her hands to her head and screamed.

It was Sadko all right, but what she saw was a gray savage mask, a quivering horror. Dozens of quills stuck out from the dog's face. They projected everywhere, circling the muzzle, thick at the nose, outlining the blue eyes with an emphasis stark and obscene.

Turning away, she buried her face in her hands.

Vague memories of old photos flashed in her mind: ancient rituals, an anthropology of pain: skin punctured by sharpened stick or blade. But this was an innocent animal, not a human initiate.

The dog had been given to them by her father, and she and John had raised it and cherished it, naming him Sadko, or Sad Company, because of his soulful blue eyes. Now she couldn't touch the creature, couldn't bear to reach out to console it. She had to steel herself, find courage, offer comfort, and she knew it—but she couldn't.. She felt horrified, but equally ashamed. This was no visitation; only a chance encounter of their poor dog with a very real porcupine. *Mila, get with it,* she told herself, *think of something!*

Then Sadko moved, like a plant that had grown a face.

She gasped and stumbled away into the next room, found the tray and bottles on the old pine table and swallowed a few shots of cognac, then gave way to a fit of interminable coughing.

She closed her eyes and stood still for long seconds. Then she struggled back to the kitchen where the phone was. The dog crouched and writhed in one corner.

She found their phone book on a nearby shelf, and frantically turned the pages, looking for the number of their vet.

The dog dragged himself across the floor, moving unsteadily, close the doorway. Did he want to go out? The day seemed to be darkening, or did she imagine it? If only John would come now. If only her father were here.

She could not bear the sight of the animal a second longer. Somehow she got the doors open, feeling the harsh wind on her face as relief. The dog seemed to read her revulsion, and slipped out before she could reach down to caress and console him.

She watched him creep and slide across the driveway and disappear in the drifting snow; he seemed to be heading for the barn. She turned back to the kitchen, swaying a little at each step. She was prone to fainting fits and struggled to pull herself together. For a moment she thought she would be sick. She reached for the phone, found the

vet's number and dialed. It rang for what seemed
ages. She cleared her throat and tried to get her
thoughts straight. At last a woman's voice, smooth
and mechanical, came on:

*"Thank you for calling Dr. Davis. At the moment
the doctor is out on an important call. Please leave a
message after the tone and we will return your call
as soon as the doctor is available."*

"Dr. Davis!" she said, and stopped. It was no
good; how could she tell him she needed him? She
had no car, and no idea when John would come
back. Sadko had vanished into the storm. It was
hopeless.

She hung up the phone and fetched herself
another brandy. The afternoon was wearing on. She
went back to the kitchen, turned down the stew she
was making for John, then collapsed at the table.

She didn't know what she should do. Her city
friends were few and too far away. Her country
neighbours, she knew, scorned her as a useless
snob of a woman who had no children, didn't go to
church, and slept with any man she fancied.

She was alone, but she couldn't have John
coming back to find the dog missing and hurt. He
would go into a rage and shout at her. He would
call her names, and if she answered back, he would

attack her. They had slugged it out more than once and both had suffered bruises and broken bones.

She had foolishly let the dog out and now she would have to go and find him. That should pacify John; he'd see she'd done her best, and wouldn't blame her. She had to admit it, her shrink was right about one thing: John was very like her father: he could be charming and sweet, but had a mean streak in him; he was quick to judge and quick to anger, and sometimes could be violent. She picked up her father's card from the counter and shoved it quickly into a drawer.

The clock said half past four. It would get dark very quickly. The snow was still coming down. From another drawer she fetched a flashlight, threw on an old barn coat, and pushed her way out and into the storm.

She was ashamed of her weakness, whimpering a little and feeling sorry for herself as she fought her way through the blowing snow. Gusts of wind showered drifts from the barn roof. The old building rose up like an ancient ship beached forever in the bleak farm earth. Despite her country childhood and her father's pleasure in such buildings, Mila had mixed feelings about them, and her time with Ronnie had only deepened her unease.

She pushed open the big door and switched the lights on. The air stank of dried-out dung and wet animals. It was chilly, too, and quite dim: the stalls and corners, and the recesses of the lofts were full of shadows. The old boards creaked in the wind, and in places snow had blown in through the cracks.

She peered around, aiming the flashlight, and soon found the dog. He hadn't really hidden, but lay half out of sight underneath a broken work table near some rotten old bales. The flashlight beam revealed his misery; he struggled, panting and seemingly helpless, rubbing his muzzle with ill-effect and obvious pain on the heaped straw. Mila sensed that he was ashamed of his predicament, but wanted her help, but what could she do? Someone would have to hold him and she would need pliers to get the quills out.

She went over, sat down beside the dog, and gently stroked him.

A car's engine sounded nearby, in the driveway.

She jumped up. *"John!"* she cried aloud. *Relief at last,* she thought, John was safe and could help her. She hurried to one of the nearby windows, wiped at the dusty pane, and peered out.

Her heart sank. She saw the vehicle clearly. A red pickup, Ronnie's truck, turning round in the driveway.

As it swung round its lights made an arc in the gloom; darkness was coming on. And she felt that moment as if a weight of darkness had fallen on her shoulders.

She watched in misery as her lover pulled up beside the kitchen entrance. She could see him through the cab window, climbing out. He paused on the doorstep, near the old pump, and after a moment or two pushed open the kitchen doors. She was angry; did he think he had the right?

Minutes later he ducked out of the doorway, came around his truck and peered across at the barn. He must have seen the lights there. He smiled and walked across toward the front of the barn.

She backed away from the window, brushed at her barn-coat and her hair. She felt ill and ugly, and above all, vulnerable. Why was he coming here to find her? They hadn't talked in a month or more. How did he know she was in the barn? She might have been out with the car, and John here.

The big barn door creaked; he came out of the shadows and saw her. He was smiling his ironical smile and looked trim and attractive. She'd forgotten how broad his shoulders were, and his sturdiness. Yet she wished she could make him disappear.

He came close, still smiling and said to her: "What

are you doing in here? Did you get an idea I'd be coming?"

Suddenly furious at his insinuation, she stood back mutely and pointed at the dog. He walked forward, bent over and examined Sadko.

He got up and glanced at her. She recognized the tenderness, the desire in his look. She had seen it so often and it was there again, but controlled and guarded.

At last she found her voice and told him: "I was trying to get the dog inside. He ran over here. I want him to be inside when John comes. John will come soon. Why are you here?"

"Oh, something made me do it. That dog needs a vet. Would you like me to drive you over to Braddock?"

"I don't want you to drive me anywhere. I just want you to go."

His smile tensed a little. "Don't pretend you don't like me and want me. I know you too well. You always play the cold bitch, but underneath—it's a little different."

He moved closer. She backed away, fearful that he would touch her. She didn't trust herself to fight him off, though she wanted him gone, and right away.

"I figure you must be tired of that other guy by now. Chop Suey, I mean, after a while you get tired of it."

"What the hell are you talking about?"

"Oh, I saw your friend from town. You can fool your husband but not me. I was watching a couple of times. I saw him driving in and out. He didn't stay too long. Short measure, I guess. I know what was going on, though. Nice-looking guy—from a distance. You wanted a change of colour, a nice little pal to play with, is that it? I thought we had something better. I saved up a lot of cash to take you away from here."

"You're insulting. Don't you dare insult me. I was weak, I gave in to you. You were nice enough, but it's over. I've told you that already. I don't want to talk to you again. You call John and tell him you're not coming to work here anymore. And don't talk to me about other people. It's none of your goddamned business what I do."

He was silent, his face wore a faint cold smile. He gave her a passionate look, but took a step backward. He seemed perplexed and uncertain. His ironical manner had vanished.

He seemed suddenly to decide something, fixed her with a serious look and said: "You're edgy about that husband of yours showing up. Well, if that's all that's bothering you, you may not have to worry...."

Her heart beat fast as she waited for him to finish.

"I was driving over near the main highway and saw your car—and I made sure it was your car—wrapped around a tree. You should be getting a phone call about now. Maybe you should wait over in the house. But I'd be careful if I were you. If he survived, I mean. One of these days that husband of yours might work out the math and go after you."

"You bastard! You dare to tell me all this. I don't believe you!"

She burst into tears, but he was unyielding. He shrugged his shoulders and started to turn away. "I'm telling you the truth. I'm sorry, but it's a fact. I'll come for you anytime if you want me," he promised, "I'll give you everything you want and you'll forget these half-men. You've been wasting your time for too long with these jokers."

He turned abruptly and made his way quickly from the barn. She stood watching him, trembling, unable to think, the tears running down her cheeks.

John, she thought. *Oh, no, please!*

The car door slammed and the pickup went grinding and roaring down their driveway.

She fell down on the dusty floor and lay there,

eyes closed, her heart beating fast, for uncountable minutes.

She felt lost; her life flashed before her: an inner drama, sustained, inescapable, absurd. What was she doing here? Blinded by love, she had persuaded John to share what she imagined would be an idyllic country life. But her sixties idealism with its myth of simplicity had deluded her. Her father, with his roots in the country, had ended up in the suburbs, but she, foolishly, had tried to go back, to connect to a life that no longer existed. But she had few appropriate skills and no community, and in the country she was powerless, and alone.

She struggled up; she had to escape from this. She would insist that they sell the farm, that they move back to the city as soon as possible. She wanted to work, she wanted friends; she wanted children. She would leave John if she had to, but she must start afresh; she must change her life.

At last, slowly, she got up and crept out of the barn. Halfway across the driveway she realized that she hadn't checked Sadko or closed the barn door. But she had no strength to go back; her infidelities, begun in that barn, had brought her too much suffering. She never wanted to go in there again.

Now she was looking for a police number. Should

she call 911? And if John had been hurt, why didn't they call her? Their car "wrapped around a tree." Had Ron been lying to her, exaggerating everything out of his hurt? Had John had an accident at all?

She would take one nip of the cognac, then call 911. She would find out the truth.

She walked into the middle room, the big sitting room, and stepped over to the pine table to get the drink. From there she could see out the window, across the fields, to the road that led to the main highway and to town. And just then, for the first time that day, in the darkness, and through the billowing snow, she saw lights, the big flashing lights of a police patrol. At the same time a siren sounded, quite recognizably, although muffled by the murmuring wind. She stopped and listened again. Sirens were never heard in the country, not on their lonely road.

She dropped her glass, ran back into the kitchen, and started out the door. The police were coming to tell her something, and she had to meet them to forestall it. She had a sudden crazy notion that if she ran to them and hushed them up, they couldn't bring her any evil news. "O Daddy," she cried out as she prepared to meet them, "please help me stop them, or turn back time, please make things all right again, and don't let John be hurt!"

She stepped across the porch and watched the flashing lights as the vehicle turned into their driveway. At that moment her telephone rang. It startled her, but she didn't want that, she wanted to talk to someone face to face.

She stood paralyzed between the two signals, breathing heavily, feeling herself nearly ready to panic. The door slammed behind her and a chill blast punished her cheeks and brow. She swallowed hard and tried to think.

She walked slowly down the driveway toward the flashing lights. The storm was still heavy. The roads must be very bad. Ron must have been telling the truth. Why hadn't she heard from John? He always seemed to call her when she needed him. She'd never given him enough credit for that. Or for a few other things. She was sad, and she remembered that blazing summer day and the hard pole slamming down on his tractor fender.

He might have died then. She stopped for a moment, shivering, and realized that she might be with someone else now, or living all alone. It was hard to imagine, and deep down, she knew she didn't want anyone else; she wanted John.

As for her, she might have died too, jumping out

of that car. He would have missed her, too, she knew that. Maybe they led charmed lives, but she didn't think so. She knew she'd have to tell him about her lovers, and he might leave her then. He might even kill her.

The phone call, the lights flashing down at the end of the driveway meant nothing. They were the superficial signals of the dangers facing two lives bound so closely together. She and John had taken a false road and now they had to choose the right one, the true path to the future. She'd change, she'd prove herself, and make him do the same. He couldn't fail to appear now. She needed him; he needed her. Like all true lovers, they were stubborn at heart. "To battle through one's troubles," she had read somewhere, "is to get in touch with your destiny, to take charge of your future."

She walked down the driveway and stopped, still several yards from the stationary police car. *Take charge of your future?* She didn't feel in charge of anything. The snow, caught in the headlights, drifted down.

A full minute passed. Then two policemen got out of their hulking car, and stood leaning on the open doors. They glanced at her, then exchanged a brief look. One of them turned and called to someone in the car.

She closed her eyes and made a wish. When she heard a familiar voice she looked up. Her husband was waving to her. He had stepped from the police car and was walking unsteadily toward her, a tall wraith-like figure lit by the flickering lights. She ran to meet him; she had something very important to tell him.. Their car, she assumed, must be wrecked. But they needed it, and right now. They would have to do something about that poor wounded dog. They'd have to drive, and talk, and take on their duties together.

She waited for his smile, his familiar greeting. If only this storm, this punishing weather, would go away.

Afterword

Although the settings vary, these stories are almost all based on aspects of the lives I've encountered while living and working in the eastern USA and Canada. My overriding interest is in people, and how they deal with their own compulsions, or face the inevitable changes that existence forces on all of us. As a reader I've found that few things can match the fascination of reading a writer who understands and conveys the changes and challenges that ordinary people contend with day after day, whatever larger issues may surround and sometimes plague them. Although I'm also intrigued by science fiction, fantasy, horror and historical narratives, writers such as Willa Cather, Knut Hamsun, Ivan Bunin,

Mikail Bulgakov and D.H. Lawrence, all masters of the significant everyday moment, are among my lifetime favourites.

Several of these stories have been published, often in slightly different versions, in American and Canadian literary magazines, and a few were broadcast on radio. The spellings, I fear, embody both U.S. and Canadian English formats. In fact, I have chosen the spelling forms I like best and mixed them to my satisfaction, without opting for one national style or the other. These stories are based on what I've seen of life in the "territory" I've mostly occupied, and on lives I have struggled to understand; nonetheless, this is a work of fiction, and any close resemblance of the events and persons depicted here to real people and events, is purely coincidental.

Also by Tom Henighan

SELECTED PUBLISHED FICTION

Tourists from Algol ((1983)

The Well of Time (1988)

Strange Attractors (1991)

Viking Quest (2001)

Mercury Man (2004)

Viking Terror (2006)

Demon in My View (2007)

Doom Lake Holiday (2009)

Nightshade (2010)

SELECTED PUBLISHED NON-FICTION

The Presumption of Culture (1996)

Ideas of North (1997)

The Maclean's Companion to Canadian Arts and
Culture (2000)

Coming of Age in Arabia (2005)

Vilhjalmur Stefansson, Arctic Adventurer (2009)

POETRY

Home Planet (1994)

Time's Fools (2010)

The Fire Lessons (2016)